WINGS OF DECEPTION

VICTORIA PAULEY

Contents

This one goes out to anyone who's ever felt like an outsider. Being different and unique isn't a bad thing, and the people who make you question your worth don't deserve your time. You're perfect just the way you are. Be unique. Be weird. Be different.
Be you.

Author's Note

Wings of Deception has been in my head for some time now and I'm thrilled to finally share it with you. While this is not a dark romance, the characters in this series all need to overcome their own issues. Some of these issues may hit close to home so please read the list below before diving in.

-This book features an FMC who struggles to fit in. She's bullied and ridiculed for being different (not by the main love interests).

-Instances of prejudice between the different types of angels.

-Open door sex.

-Episodes of PTSD from past trauma with flashbacks of a witnessed death

-Mention of the prior death of a parent.

-A difficult relationship with family.

Silver City University Map

1

HAYLIEL

R *un, Hayliel.*

I push my legs as fast as they'll go, rushing past fancy stalls with decadent aromas and the angry merchants that run them, pivoting to avoid their grabby hands before turning left down an alley. I mentally pat myself on the back for stuffing my long brown hair into a hat. It means there's one less feature for them to identify me by if this goes sideways and one less thing they can grab hold of. Footsteps pound on the cobblestones behind me, followed by shouts of "Stop her!" but I won't let them stop me.

Change is a scary thing. It doesn't care about fear or denial, it just is. It's a sentient being you can try to fight off but, in the end, it's inevitable. Things can't stay the same forever, no matter how much we may want them to.

That's why I've been reckless. If change wants to take me, well ... I'll serve up some of that myself. There's a market a few blocks away from our apartment, one that sells delicious pastries, silken gowns, and all the baubles a Pure-born girl could dream of. Despite living so close, I've never ventured inside. I've always been too afraid of what might happen.

But today, with all its change glaring me in the face, I put aside my fear. If they're going to force us from our home, then I'm not leaving without a taste of their decadent desserts. Too bad someone figured out I didn't belong. The market is only for the Pure, after all. And I'm anything but.

I press on, my shoes splashing through murky puddles as I make it to the end of the alley and pull myself up on top of the massive trash can. Gone are the sweet and savory scents of the market, replaced by moldy food and the stench of the poor. I could have just unfurled my wings and flown, avoided the grimy, filth-covered bin, but that's too dangerous. There are too many watchful eyes out here, and my discolored wings aren't exactly something people fail to notice. Instead, I jump high, grab the metal drainpipe on the side of the building, and climb.

Despite the warm day, the metal is cold beneath my fingers. Bits of rust stick to my hands as I make my ascent, but I'm at the top quickly, even with my short stature.

"She went down there. Don't let her get away!"

I hold my breath, trying to focus on the task at hand instead of the approaching guards. Not bothering to look down, I use every ounce of strength I have to pull myself up one last time and collapse on the roof. I just lie there. Tiny tendrils of brown hair have escaped my hat and now stick to my face, but I'm too scared to fix them. *Deep breaths, Hayles.*

Sound echoes from the alley as multiple angels rush in. If any of them saw me climb up here, I'll be so fucking screwed. All it will take is one of them flying up to check the roof and they'll find me. My overconfidence from earlier turns to ash in my mouth. *Fuck! What had I been thinking?*

An argument breaks out below, and I move, taking advantage of the noise to muffle my own. With only a few steps between me and the far side of the roof, hope flares bright in my stomach.

Then comes the flap of wings.

The rustle of feathers.

My heartbeat skyrockets, pumping wildly until the tingling in my chest extends to my hands and feet. If they find me, what will they do to me and my family? I can't let them get caught up in this mess, not on our last day together.

I jump.

Thankfully, I've spent enough time up here to know the drop from one roof to the next won't cause any damage, but it isn't exactly pleasant either. I'm close enough to the safety of my room that, if I were lucky, I'd make it. But I know better than to rely on Lady Luck. That fickle bitch has never once shown up for me.

I press close to the wall, my pale olive skin helping me to blend with the shadow of the building, and listen intently to the angels in the sky. Their boots thump down above me — the sound amplified by stone — and I suck in a sharp breath. Covering my mouth, I wait. And wait. And wait some more.

Shit. How much longer are they going to look for me? My limbs stiffen, urging me to move from this spot, but I stay put. *Just a little longer.*

Finally I hear, "Clear! Our little flier is long gone."

Relief floods my system, and I can breathe a little easier now that my pursuers are gone, but I still wait a few more minutes before allowing myself to move. I can't wait to see the look on my parents' faces when they see what I brought them. Giddy with excitement, I grin as I squeeze through a narrow passage between buildings.

Once I make it through, I lower myself off the side until my feet find the solid bar of my window. *Almost home free, Hayles.*

Reality crashes into me as I tug my window up and slip into my now-empty room. The boxes I'd packed earlier are gone, and only the faint scent of lemon lingers. Mom must have cleaned it while I was out. Turning my back on the room, I blink away the tears threatening to spill over. When I open them again, my determined blue gaze stares back at me from the reflection in the window.

A month ago we'd found an eviction notice pinned to our apartment door, notifying us that in thirty days we'd have to find somewhere else to live. A Pure family now needs the home I've lived in for my entire life, and we had no choice but to give it up.

As much as I want to, we can't fight it. At least, not without making things worse. So, my parents packed up their belongings and prepared to make a new home.

I pull the strap of my bag from my shoulders, wincing at the ache running through them. I consider giving in to the need to stretch my wings, but I'm so used to hiding them, I easily shake it off and settle for inspecting the goodies inside my bag instead before heading to find my parents.

Mom's in the kitchen, scrubbing the now-empty cupboards. "Where have you been, Haylie-bear?" She uses the nickname I've always hated, but now I fear I'll never hear it again after today.

Shrugging off the sadness, I force a smile. "Well, we hadn't really celebrated the move or my enrollment yet, so ..."

Dad walks in, securing a fresh roll of tape to the dispenser. When he finishes, he musses up my hair and I roll my eyes.

"You're always going on about how things happen for a reason and there's always a silver lining, so I'm *trying* to embrace it. Here!" I pull three massive pastries from my bag and hand them each one.

Mom's eyes grow wide as she takes the flaky dessert from me, and Dad only chuckles when he takes his.

"You know, this day wouldn't have felt complete without tasting one of these bad boys, kiddo," Dad says before stuffing it in his mouth.

"Hayliel ..." Mom counters, looking torn on whether she should be upset or pleased.

"It's fine, Mom. I got away without using my wings. Plus, in a few hours I'll be long gone and no one will see me again." *Yup. I went there. What can I say? I'm a real mood killer.*

Ignoring the sad look in her eyes, I take a large bite of the pastry and damn near collapse on the floor. Holy shit. This might be the best thing I've ever tasted. Slivered almonds mixed in some type of paste on a flaky dough with powdered sugar? Yes, please!

"Has Dina told you much about the food at SCU? If they have these, I might have to enroll myself." Dad licks the powdered sugar from his fingers as he stares at the last half of Mom's pastry like he might just steal it.

"If they have these, then she's been holding out on me," I reply with a mouthful of food. Dina enrolled last year after acing the entrance exam, and though we haven't spent as much time together as we used to, at least I'll already have a friend at school. She knows me. Every fear and hope, even my secrets. With her by my side, I can get through anything.

"Your principal assured me you'd receive a brand-new slate today. You know you can call us anytime, right?" Mom sets down her pastry and pulls me into a hug.

With her distracted, Dad reaches for the last piece of her dessert but, as expected, he doesn't make it that far. "Don't you dare," Mom scolds, though there's no bite in her tone.

With one last squeeze, she turns to her pastry and picks it up before striding closer to Dad. "You can have it, but only if I feed you."

Gag.

Of all the things I'll miss about living here with my parents, this definitely isn't one of them.

A short while later, I take a deep, calming breath before opening my eyes and staring at the wrought-iron gate in front of me. Only a few blocks from where I grew up, it shouldn't have taken me so long to arrive, yet I couldn't help but drag my feet.

This is it. Once I pass that barrier, there's no turning back. Not that I could turn back now, but denial rides my ass hard. I don't know what I envisioned my life to be, but it isn't this. This place has always been a fairy tale, one I never considered would accept me, let alone allow me in on a scholarship.

But I guess that's what life is like when the world constantly makes you feel unworthy. You start to believe it.

A shiver races down my spine, some odd sense of foreboding that I don't really want to investigate. As optimistic as my parents are, I find it hard to adopt the same attitude. Maybe that's because as much as I try to live a glass-half-full kind of life, something always knocks it over, spilling the contents and leaving it empty.

Shaking my head, I grab the handle of my suitcase and let go of those negative thoughts. I'm here now. It's time to learn my powers, accept my fate, and hopefully uncover why my wings are so different.

With a confident sway to my hips, I step past the threshold and into my life at Silver City University.

2

HAYLIEL

The cement beneath my feet turns to stone and leads toward a pristine building in the distance. Its white walls sparkle in the late afternoon sun, and the scent of the ocean fills the air, making it feel like I've escaped Silver City altogether. *Beautiful.*

On the path up ahead, a single Pure angel waits for me with a smile. I look back once and shudder as reality sinks in. Everything is about to change. After years of dreaming about SCU, I finally have the chance to attend, and I won't let anything stand in my way. *I only hope it's not just Dina that accepts me.*

"Hayliel?" the man asks as I approach, his white wings tucked in casually at his back.

"That's me."

Like all angels, his face holds a youthful glow, but something about him gives off the impression that he's far older than one would expect.

"I'm Professor Castiel, and I'm here to officially welcome you to our great school." He opens his arms with a flourish, presenting the school behind him. A lock of hair escapes his ponytail, but he quickly tucks it behind his ear. "We'll stop by the office first to grab your class schedule and other paperwork, then we'll take a quick tour of the grounds on our way to your house. Are you excited?"

I nod, my smile bright as the tension leaves my body for what might be the first time in days. Something about his presence offers a sense of safety and security I don't often feel with anyone outside of my parents. Especially not with a Pure. "I'm a little nervous too, if I'm honest."

His grin brightens further, and he motions for us to continue on the path. "Oh, there's nothing to be nervous about. We might have high expectations for our students, but just keep your grades up and you'll be fine. In fact, you'll probably find that life at SCU is quite similar to how you lived before."

I laugh, my eyes trained on the glimmering building in front of us. "I very much doubt that."

He doesn't respond, releasing a chuckle as we walk in comfortable silence, the only sound coming from my small suitcase as it rolls over stone.

The path ahead branches out in several directions. On the left, large marble Pure angels loom over us, casting eerie shadows at our feet. Along the right are massive stone-carved books, opened to a page with delicately drawn words chiseled into it. My parents would love this.

My chest squeezes, but I try not to let it show.

We don't turn in either direction, continuing straight toward the imposing white building. That must be where the office is. *I hope they give me a damn map. This place is enormous!*

"There are three houses within school grounds—Power, Knowledge, and Fallen. The house of Power is over there," he says, pointing to where the angel statues line the path. "And, as I'm sure you can guess, the house of Knowledge is down the path to our right."

My mind churns, trying desperately to memorize everything.

As if sensing my train of thought, Professor Castiel speaks up. "Don't worry. You'll receive a map along with your class schedule. And one can never truly be lost with the power of flight on their side, hmm?"

I smile, and my shoulder blades tense with the need to free my wings, but I keep them firmly locked inside. I'd like to meet a few students before I announce to the world just how much of an oddball I truly am.

As we approach the enormous set of white doors, a thought occurs to me. "What about the third house?"

"Ah, yes. The house of the Fallen is beyond the main hall and past the other campus buildings. You'll find it's not as easily accessible as the rest, and for that I apologize. I've been trying to get them to change it up, but you know how the purists can be."

My eyes flick to his, and I almost stumble at his words.

"We're not all elitists, you know. I do prefer my books over the company of others, and it's not hard to guess why." He winks, letting his wings retreat into his body before rushing forward to open the door.

"Thank you." I'm completely in awe of this strange man who seems so different from the Pure teachers I'd met at my last school.

The silent feud between angels has been ongoing since before Mom and Dad were born. My now-estranged grandparents told me stories as a child that feel more like fairy tales than our history. The Pure against the Fallen. No one seems to care that our wing color is decided at birth. It's completely random, not based on any oracle or prophecy. A Pure angel could be the cruelest being of all and still have snowy-white feathers while a Fallen angel could be a fucking saint and still get shunned by society.

Then there's me: A complete and utter anomaly who doesn't fit into any of the neat little boxes that society makes.

If most of these angels are like Professor Castiel, maybe my time here won't be so bad after all.

Once inside, we follow signs for the office until we turn toward a large desk and Professor Castiel explains who I am. While he speaks to the man behind the desk, I try to stay present, but several pictures along the back wall catch my eye. The dates along the bottom of each photo tell which year they were taken, and a choir of angels takes flight in my belly. Regardless of wing color or status, every single photo depicts smiling students who seem genuinely happy. *Will it be like this for me?*

Hearing my name, I tear my gaze from the photos and sign a piece of paper, not entirely sure what it is I'm agreeing to, but I'd rather not explain why I wasn't paying attention. With a loud *thunk*, the school receptionist drops a thick binder on the desk in front of me, along with a backpack filled to the brim.

"Why don't you wait outside, I'll just be a moment," Professor Castiel says, pointing toward a different door than the one we entered.

"Of course, thank you both." I pick up my things, excitement bubbling at the prospect of finding out what's inside. As I step out the back door, my breath stalls. I hadn't thought this campus could get any better, but it turns out I was wrong.

A tall building stands off in the distance, looking like the tower one would lock a princess inside of before her knight came to save her. Beyond it, there's a large cliff that spans almost the entire right side of campus with a waterfall pouring from the top. A massive fountain sits on my left, bubbling water spewing from several points, and the sound of it relaxes me almost immediately. Angels lounge near the fountain, some with their wings out and others without, but all of them have smiles on their faces. I can't stop the hope blossoming inside me.

"Breathtaking, isn't it?" Professor Castiel asks, taking it all in along with me.

"Beyond anything I could have imagined. I didn't expect the school grounds to be so large." I hold tight to the binder, barely feeling the weight of my new belongings, and haul my suitcase along behind us as we head toward a large grove of trees. Every place I look holds something interesting, even if it's as plain as a cabin on the horizon or a crop of colorful flowers.

The professor is talking — something about the many buildings and activities the school runs — and I should listen, but as we approach the thick forest, two large stone carvings of black wings on either side of the path grab my attention. This must be the way to the Fallen house. *My new home.*

Something draws me toward the nearest statue, forcing me to reach out and touch it. Immediately, my skin tingles and a sinister sense of foreboding fills my veins. *What the fuck?*

"Come along, Hayliel. Just a little farther," Professor Castiel calls from ahead of me, and I rush to catch up.

The path takes us through a forest, where birds chirp and leaves rustle in the soft breeze, yet the world seems darker beneath the thick canopy. Corpses of fallen trees are strewn through the undergrowth with brightly colored mushrooms growing around them. Some trunks have faces on them, eyes that watch as we get closer to the end of the path. I breathe in deep, letting the rich, earthy scents calm me a little.

A dark castle looms over the end of the path, and I can't help but gasp. "Wow." The only words that come to mind are gothic chic. Dina had described this to me when she first started, but I never actually believed she lived in a fucking castle. She's going to freak when she finds out I'm finally here.

"Just wait until you see inside." He peers down at his watch, a frown forming on his brow before he grabs a slip of paper from his pocket. "I almost forgot. Here is your room number. I'm afraid this is where I leave you, unless you'd like some assistance?"

He hands me the small piece of neatly folded paper, but I don't open it. "No, it's alright. I can make it from here. Thank you for everything, Professor."

"I look forward to seeing you blossom at this school, Miss Hayliel. Should you need anything, you can find all faculty contacts in that binder there, but your house captain, Ezekiel, is one of the best. Good luck!" His wings burst free from his back, slipping through the slits made specifically for our kind, and he flies away.

Ezekiel. Something about his name sends a jolt of energy down my spine, one I try to shake off by reading my room number. 7-0-2.

I look up at the imposing castle before me, my frayed nerves wishing I'd asked Professor Castiel for help. *Now is not the time for wallowing in self-pity, Hayles.*

Slipping the paper into my pocket, I open the binder and flip through the pages, hoping to find a map of this house somewhere within. It shouldn't be too hard to find my room, but as nervous as I am today, I'd rather be overprepared.

A gorgeous man drops from the sky, dark hair blowing across his face. I can't help the shriek that escapes me as he lands directly in front of me, his black wings spread wide behind him.

Yum. Who the hell is this guy?

Before I can stop myself, I reach a hand toward his wings, desperate to feel the soft feathers beneath my fingers. He snaps them shut, and my eyes immediately jump to his face. Piercing green eyes meet mine, assessing me as a smirk grows on his too handsome face. *Shit. What the fuck was that?*

"Um, hi," I say, breathlessly. As if I could be any lamer. He doesn't answer, only watches me through green eyes as I watch him in return.

His outfit looks more like a uniform than a style choice, with a symbol stitched into the fabric on the left side. Some combination of A and G woven together over a pair of dual blades. Something about it feels oddly familiar, but I can't quite place where I've seen it before. I try not to stare at the rest of him for fear that I might start drooling, because holy shit. This guy clearly works out. Even his muscles have muscles.

I bet he'd have zero issues holding my weight while screwing my brains out. *Whoa, where the hell did that come from?*

As if hearing my thoughts, the man chuckles, stepping closer until my breath catches and my entire body tingles with anticipation. "Welcome to the house of the Fallen," he whispers, trailing a hand down my arm, and all I can do is stand there, slack jawed and wide eyed. I'm utterly frozen, completely enthralled by his touch. "Let me take this."

What the hell is he even talking about? Whatever it is, he can have it. Especially if it's me. He can definitely have that.

It's only when he steps away that I realize he's taken my suitcase and is already hauling it toward the front door.

"You coming or what?" he calls over his shoulder, and I swear I hear laughter in his voice.

"Hold up! Who are you and why the hell should I trust you with my things?" I probably should have said something earlier, but I'm weak.

This guy may be hotter than sin, but that doesn't mean I can trust him. Is he helping because he wants something, or is he actually just a nice guy? *If those even exist ...*

He doesn't reply, only shooting me a backward glance before stepping through the front door of the Fallen house. Heat warms my cheeks, but I shake it off and pretend the mortally embarrassing moment didn't happen before following him inside.

A grand staircase stands front and center, winding up and seeming to go on forever. The railing is thick and looks exactly like the ones children slide down in the movies from Earth. *Note to self: slide down the banister at least once before graduation.*

"Do you like it?" a dark voice says from the corner where he stands with my things.

"I love it." I sigh, turning to take in the rest of the area. "Who are you again, and why are you holding my things hostage?"

"There are far prettier things I'd rather take hostage, if that's on the table." He steps forward, and I swallow past the lump in my throat because holy shit ... Did he just say he wants to take me hostage?

"I'm Ezekiel, house captain of the Fallen. And who are you?"

So this was who Professor Castiel mentioned earlier. I'm glad as shit that he's not here to witness whatever the hell is currently happening between us.

"I'm Hayliel."

"Pretty name for a pretty angel. Let me show you around your new home while we get better acquainted."

His voice shifts when he says those last two words, darkening somehow and tugging on the very essence of my core. *Fuck, he's good.*

"Student lounge areas are over here," he says, motioning me through a doorway and into a wide room filled with students. There's an entire wall which appears to be a screen, playing a movie I've never seen before, and several angels sit on the long sectional with popcorn and chips. A little further into the room is a pool table, ping-pong table, and an entire shelf of board games.

As we walk through, all eyes are on Ezekiel. Just how popular is this dude? The guys raise their glasses in salute, while the girls shoot him lust-filled glances that make me want to press myself against him and claim him as mine.

We keep walking, leaving the student lounge and heading down a long corridor.

"We also have a small library here, though it's nothing like what's inside the Knowledge house." He opens the door, letting me look inside the comfortable space. There are small tables set up, a few couches, a roaring fireplace, and at least two dozen large bookshelves. Fuck. *If this is small, I can't wait to see what the other houses' libraries look like.*

Ezekiel notices the joy on my face. "Our collection is pretty varied, so whether you like history or smut, you'll find it all in there."

My mouth pops open, and I swing my gaze to his. The devilish half smirk on his face tells me the smut is no joke, so I try to play it off like I *don't* want to rush inside to find whatever hot books he mentioned and binge read them. "Good to know," is all I manage before turning away and heading farther down the hall, leaving him behind. *Is it smart to leave the tour guide who holds my belongings behind? Nope. But I don't claim to be very smart.*

He catches up easily, pointing out other rooms along the hall. The main level has shared bathrooms, with each dorm housing their own private ones as well. This floor also sports a small kitchenette with beverages and snacks. I'll find anything with substance in the main hall cafeteria, and after what Dina told me, I definitely won't go hungry.

"This house is the smallest of the three and only has eight floors. As house leader, I'm at the top. The binder from the office should include your room number. Can I see it?"

I take the slip of paper from my pocket and pass it over. As I wait for him to read it, my mind whirls while I try to absorb everything. I'm going to live in a fucking castle! How cool is that? Since entering the grounds of this gorgeous school, I thought I might see Dina, but not yet. She's most likely off hanging with her friends, lounging somewhere epic that I haven't discovered yet.

My gaze returns to Ezekiel as his face lights up, eyes widening slightly.

"What?" I ask, my voice trembling as terrible thoughts fly through my mind. What if there was a mistake and I can't stay here? Would I end up stranded and alone or forced to live with my parents in their new home?

"Scholarship students are usually on the first floor as those are the smallest rooms, but it looks like someone must have bumped you up. Let me guess, Professor Castiel was your tour guide today? You're on the seventh floor."

"Why would he do that?" I stammer, completely taken aback by his kindness.

"Why does anyone do anything?" he counters with a dark grin. "Come on, I'll show you to your room."

I only realize we're headed back outside when we reach the front door. Ezekiel already has it open, my suitcase in hand, and I just stand there like an idiot. "Uh, isn't the seventh floor that way?" I ask, pointing at the stairs.

"It is. Exceptional detective skills, Hayliel. While you *can* get to the seventh floor by the stairs, I much prefer to fly." He shoots me a wink that has my toes practically curling in my sneakers, but the roiling storm in my stomach distracts me from all else.

I can't expose myself this soon. It's my first day and I've only met two freaking angels!

"No," I blurt out. Panic consumes me as Ezekiel raises an eyebrow in question. "What I mean is that I'd rather take the stairs this time to familiarize myself with the layout. Otherwise, I'll probably fuck up the floor count and accidentally enter the wrong room, only to wind up catching someone shaving their asshole, and then I'll be stuck with that image forever." Fucking fuck. I'm babbling like a fool, but the goddamn word-vomit won't stop. *Shaved assholes, Hayles? Really?*

Thankfully, Ezekiel speaks up before I continue embarrassing myself. "Have you caught many people shaving their asshole?" His voice wavers slightly and, if I didn't know any better, I'd think he was trying to hide a laugh. "Actually, I don't want to know the answer. We'll take the stairs. I wouldn't be much of a house leader if I let you come face-to-face with someone's ham flower on your first day, now would I?"

I bark a laugh and immediately blush. *What in the seven hells was that?* I've never laughed like that in my entire freaking life. What the fuck is happening to me?

Ezekiel grabs my suitcase and moves up the stairs, checking on me every few steps and calling out which floor we're on once we hit the landing. Up and up we go, until it feels like we're in a time loop and this will be my life from now on. Damn. How in the world do the Earth folk do this? Without my immortal strength and stamina, I'd probably have died after the third floor.

The further up we go, the fewer doors there are along the hall. There's a lightness in my chest that has me on the verge of giggles as I imagine what my nearly top floor room will look like. *Just how spacious will it be?*

When we finally make it to the seventh floor, I'm more than ready to explore my new home. There are only four doors along the hall, each one marked with a silver number on the front.

Ezekiel puts my suitcase down as I reach for the door marked 7-0-2, but before I can turn the knob, his hand covers mine.

Every nerve ending lights up beneath his touch, but I don't look at him. Fuck, I *can't* look at him. For whatever reason, I don't have a single ounce of control around this guy, and I'm afraid that if I look at him when he's touching me, I won't be able to stop myself from doing something really fucking dumb.

The scent of leather wraps around me, invading my senses. Beneath it, there are hints of jasmine and musk that have me practically salivating. Fuck. They don't make men like this outside the university, at least not where I come from.

His skin is rough and warm against my wrist, the tips of his fingers caressing me in a way that sends shivers all the way to my toes. We stay this way until a loud moan from the room across the hall breaks me from the trance, and I yank my hand back.

My house leader appears completely unfazed by the exchange. "It's locked," he says, pulling a key from his pocket and handing it to me. "I have copies of every key for this building. You should have one in your binder, but if you ever lose it or have trouble accessing your room, come find me. Most students don't use the stairs because each balcony has a wing sensor. You'll find instructions to set that up in the student binder."

I nod, taking in his words while I unlock the door and push it open. He doesn't come inside, choosing instead to lean against the door frame while I take in the massive area. *My new home.*

"I've got to get cleaned up, so I'll let you get settled. Most of the students are easy to get along with, at least within the Fallen. So, as much as I see you eyeing that bed, I'd recommend mingling a little."

Giving him my full attention, I thank the Archangels that he doesn't seem to realize my thoughts on the bed had nothing to do with sleep and far more to do with *him.* "Thanks for the tour, Ezekiel," I say, handing back his key. "I won't stay locked in here, I promise."

"Good." He smiles and turns to leave, but stops before I shut the door. "Oh, and there's a start-of-term house party in two days. It's not exactly mandatory, but only the social pariahs don't go, so ... show up. Okay?"

I smile, giddy beyond belief. "Okay."

He shuts the door, and I wait a solid sixty seconds before squealing and jumping on the bed.

I don't know if the excitement will ever wear off, but once I've made a mess of the sheets, I hop off the bed and head over to the desk in the corner.

My binder sits on top, begging for me to look through it, so I do just that. What kind of person would I be if I let down this inanimate object?

I find my brand-new slate tucked inside the front pocket. It's a sleek black, with not a single fingerprint found on it, and I almost don't want to mar the device.

Powering it on, I send a quick message to Dina then set it aside and flip through the rest of the papers. I glance at the school map, noting the different campus buildings and a beach not too far from the Fallen house. Beside the main hall is an odd-looking circle of trees with a structure in the center that piques my interest, but I put that thought on the back burner before I race outside to explore. There will be time for that another day. Beneath the map is a list of extracurricular activities, a contact list for faculty, and my schedule. It's almost overwhelming. The class schedule has my fingers shaking slightly. History, Angelic Powers — finally — a few core subjects ... Wingology. Studying the one thing I'm trying to keep private in front of a whole class. I need to do this though. I knew I was going to have to add some classes I'd really rather avoid to get my answers, so I'll deal. Somehow.

An SCU catalog sits tucked into the very back, showcasing the school's branded clothing line, including the specific uniform and colors for each house. Power is purple. Knowledge is blue. And, to my surprise, Fallen is red. *Finally! No more forced black outfits for me.*

I rush over to the large closet along the wall, sad to find it empty. Do I have to purchase them separately?

A knock sounds on the door, making my heart skip a beat. Has Ezekiel come back or is it someone else?

With a deep breath, I open the door, only the hall is empty. A large box sits on the floor, and I have half a mind to leave it there. Back home, we'd never open unexpected packages. Not that we'd receive bombs or anything. Very little could hurt us. But I've seen way too many glitter bombs in my life to want to see another.

I don't bother pulling the box into my room. Instead, I rush inside to grab the pair of scissors from my desk, then open it in the hallway.

Nothing explodes and no glitter streams through the top as I peel open the flaps. Only clothes. Piles and piles of uniforms in different options, all a silvery gray with red trim. Beneath them lies other SCU branded clothes in an array of colors, including sweatpants, sweaters, T-shirts, and even a few pairs of shoes.

I pull the box inside, shutting my door and locking it from habit before throwing myself into taking every single piece out of the box and trying it on.

This might not be exactly how I expected my life to go, but if this room is any indication, I'm in for one wild ride.

3

RAPHAEL

"**S**hit, man. How am I supposed to choose?" My eyes drift over the array of food in front of me. They have everything someone might want for breakfast. From waffles and French toast, to cereal, pastries, and even an omelet station. From sweet to savory, there's a new scent at every turn.

"Who the hell said anything about choosing?" Theo laughs, grabbing one of everything and setting them on his tray.

I follow his lead and snatch up everything that looks appetizing until my plate is overflowing. Why not take advantage of the full meal plan? They built it into the steep tuition cost, so clearly they want us to use it.

Just because the Archangels considered us adults doesn't mean we've stopped growing. At least, not with all the fun we plan to have while we're here.

While Theo grabs us a table, I jog over to the row of fridges along the back wall. I might like options, but this is ridiculous. There's freshly squeezed orange juice, mixed fruit smoothies, water, and that's only in the first fridge! I grab an OJ for myself and water for Theo, but when I turn around, I almost drop both drinks and my entire damn tray. *Fuck me.*

Walking through the cafeteria door is a total fucking bombshell. She's laughing at something her friend says, and just witnessing it feels like I'm basking in a sunbeam.

I rush back to our table, keeping the new girl in my line of vision in case she tries to disappear. Theo hasn't noticed yet, too absorbed in the video on his slate to pay attention to anything going on in the cafeteria.

"Dude. The hottest girl I've ever fucking seen just walked in. A literal goddamn angel."

He smirks, though it doesn't quite reach his eyes. Sometimes Theo gets like this, hyper-focused on the news. Absolute tunnel-vision. I can't blame him for it, not after what he went through when we were young. I just wish I could do more to help.

"Let's go sit with them," I practically beg. I don't want to ditch my friend, not when he's the closest thing to a real sibling I've ever had, but something about that girl draws me in. *I have to know her.*

"Nah. I've got to finish this," he replies distractedly, his curly brown hair flopping slightly into his face. "But you go, Raph. I'll be fine. We'll catch up later."

I suck on my bottom lip, considering his offer. Theo and I have been best friends for years, so I know that when he says something, it's not just posturing. I pat him on the back, grateful that he understands. He and I can discuss whatever video has him all wound up later, but for now, I have a stunning creature to charm.

With the jitters running through my limbs, I probably look like a psychopath. I wouldn't be at all surprised to find my eyes crazed and drool pouring from my mouth, none of it for the food piled on my tray.

Before I get very far, three angels block my path. It's clear from the first glance that the blonde one in the middle calls all the shots. The other two must be her wing-women. *Shit, that's funny.* I stifle a laugh before they notice. "Raphael, is it?" the leader says, her lips somehow smiling and pouting at the same time.

"That's me, pleasure to meet you," I respond, shifting to look around them and make sure the angel I seek hasn't left yet.

"This is Seraphina," the girl to the left says.

"She's a first-year Pure from the Power house and comes from a strong, successful family of Pures," the angel to the right says.

Seraphina holds out her hand, and I stare at it for a second. What the hell am I supposed to do with that? Kiss it? I almost gag, but manage to keep my composure. We might share blond hair and white wings, but there's no fucking chance in hell that I'm telling her we share a house too. These girls give me the goddamn creeps. But I'm nothing if not kind, so I smile like I care and shake her hand.

"It's lovely to meet you all. I'm actually on my way to meet a friend though, if you'll excuse me." I sidestep around them, beelining it for the table that holds the angel who already has her claws dug into me.

I take a deep breath, trying to calm down and access the easygoing charm I've perfected as I approach my new obsession. "Is this seat taken?"

My stunning angel tilts her head back, our eyes locking instantly. She says nothing, the smile playing on her lips drawing my attention.

Her friend kicks her beneath the table. "Uh, no. Go for it. I'm Dina, this is Hayliel. What's your name?"

Hayliel ... I want to taste her name on my tongue, but more than that, I want to taste *her*. Everything around me vanishes until she's all I see. Whatever charm I might have had before now is gone, and I'm okay with it. A girl like her deserves far better than what I've given anyone else.

"I'm Raphael, but my friends call me Raph." My words are only for Hayliel. I can't seem to shift my gaze from her dark-blue eyes, fully captivated by the specks of gold and silver within their depths.

"Did you bring all that food for the table or is that all for you?" she asks, her melodic voice a touch lower than I expected.

"Well, technically when I piled it on my plate it was all for me, but if you want some, I'd be more than happy to give it to you."

She snorts a laugh, blushing as she reaches forward to steal one of the tiny pastries from my plate. While she chews, she releases a moan that shakes my entire fucking being, and I can't help the little jump my dick makes in my pants.

"They don't make food like this outside the university, I swear," she says, holding me in a trance as she licks the crumbs from her fingers.

"Damn. You truly have the voice of an angel. Do you know that?"

Her eyes flick to mine once more, her lips held in a flat line which tells me I've definitely just blown any chance I might have had.

"That was so fucking lame, dude," the other chick, Dee or maybe Dani, says, breaking the silence. "Of course she does. She's an angel. Everyone here is."

"I'm normally much more charming, I assure you." Cupping the back of my neck, I try to figure out how to salvage this fucking mess. This can't be happening. I finally meet the angel of my dreams, only to end up being the weird, creepy guy she'll likely avoid for the rest of the semester.

"You're probably just hungry." Hayliel pops a grape into her mouth, smiling at me. Anyone else would have sent me packing, but for some reason. she doesn't. It's my lucky fucking day.

"You're probably right. How about I shut up and eat, and you can tell me how you two met?" I tear my eyes from hers, forcing them to the plate of food in front of me. This is exactly the distraction I need, and if I can get them talking, maybe it'll save me from any further embarrassment. I take a healthy bite of waffle, but I barely notice the sweet flavor. I'm too distracted by the goddess in front of me to care what's in my mouth.

"Hayles and I have been best friends for years. Thank the Archangels that we wound up in the same house here. We're in—"

"On the same floor. We're neighbors." Hayliel gives her friend a look that I can't read, but I ignore it and take the opening.

"Oh, that's cool. My best friend goes here too, but we're in different houses. He's bunked at the Knowledge house, which suits him to a fucking tee."

"I hear their library is incredible! I'd like to see it someday," Hayliel replies between bites of her wrap.

I continue chewing, the waffle on my plate almost gone, while I think about her words. If she hasn't seen the library, does that mean she isn't at the Knowledge house? It's possible she just hasn't explored yet, I suppose. She isn't in the Power house, that I know for certain. With how drawn I am to her, I'd definitely have noticed.

Neither of them wears the school uniform, but that's not entirely out of the ordinary given the school year hasn't officially started yet. But the way she dodged my question makes me think she's Fallen. Not that I care either way. Society might like to separate us and play us against one another, but I'm not about that. Regardless, if she doesn't want me to know yet, I won't push it.

"I could ask my friend to show you around, if you want. But be warned ... he can literally talk about history for hours, so you might not escape."

Her eyes brighten until they damn near glow with excitement. "Oh, yes! If you don't mind, of course."

"We've gotta go, babe." Her friend stands, turning to me and smiling for what might be the first time since I sat down. "It was nice to meet you. Make sure you're eating enough food though, yeah? Helps the whole charm thing." She pats my arm, then walks off.

Hayliel stands, stealing one more pastry from my tray. "See you around, Raphael."

"No doubt about that," I reply, but she's already gone. Letting out a long sigh, I try not to let it bother me that she called me Raphael instead of Raph. It's only our first meeting. That's all. And it's not like it means she won't ever do it.

Maybe you're just hungry. I replay her words and can't help the groan that builds in my throat as I push the tray away and plant my face on the cool table. I know damn well that food has nothing to do with my odd behavior. It's her. Just being near her had all my wires crossing. Pretty angels aren't exactly uncommon. It's built into our DNA. So, what is it about her that has me so worked up?

I pick up my things and head back to Theo, avoiding Seraphina and her pushy gaggle of friends. Defeat rears its ugly head, scratching at my insides until it hurts.

He's eaten most of the food from his tray, his slate lying face down on the table, so he notices my discomfort right away.

"How did it go with the pretty angel?" he asks, watching as I collapse into the chair beside him.

"Horrible. Every ounce of game I have flew out the fucking door as soon as I got close enough. Her friend made up a glaringly obvious excuse just to get away, so I doubt she'll ever talk to me again."

"Eat, Raph. You get like this when you're hungry," Theo tells me, pushing my tray toward me.

Perking up, I meet his gaze. "I do? It's the hunger? Oh, thank the Archangels!" I devour my food, eating like a barbarian and feeling my charm refill with every swallow. *Maybe I'll get another chance!*

Theo sits up straighter, watching as I wolf down the food in front of me like a starving angel on the brink of death. "Well? What's she like?"

"She's perfect," I mumble around a mouthful of now-cold egg before swallowing. "I don't think she's in either of our houses, but she dodged the question, so I didn't pry. Her voice is pure sin, Theo. Pure fucking sin. Oh, I kind of offered that you'd show her the Knowledge house library ... maybe we can plan some sort of chance encounter or something, so it's not weird if I just show up."

He laughs. "Dude, when have I not enjoyed spending time in any library? Of course. Once she's settled, let's invite her to hang out with us. I'd like to meet the angel who has you so wound up."

A lightbulb goes off in my mind. "Brilliant idea! Once I'm no longer hungry, I'm sure I'll have a few good ones of my own to contribute too."

With a friend like Theo, this disaster of a day might just turn around.

4

EZEKIEL

Start-of-term parties are my favorite, partly because I can switch off from worrying about demons, but mostly because they're one of the few times we Fallen have our own thing. And as house leader, it means that I can plan this exactly how I want. *Having no one to answer to sure has its perks.*

Our parties last year were lame, and I don't just mean boring. I mean full on everyone-brings-their-favorite-textbook lame. When the old leader stepped down before graduation, the rest of the student population picked me as his replacement, and I've been making changes ever since.

Tonight's the last night of freedom before term starts, when every single student here will fight to keep their spot at SCU.

I'm no different. I'm here to follow in my father's footsteps by joining the Assassins' Guild, and I'll do everything in my power not to let him down. Music blares from the speakers, and the neon body paint that coats our clothes and skin glows beneath the flickering black lights.

There are so many angels here, but I'm searching for one in particular. Hayliel hasn't shown up yet, and I'm starting to worry that maybe she won't come at all. I shouldn't care. She's only one angel in a sky full of other angels, but then why can't I stop hunting for her?

With the back doors swung wide, I can see most of the students outside dancing or lounging on the plush sectionals along the deck. It looks like a damn rainbow out there, gleaming bodies grinding against one another to the beat of the music.

As Fallen, it always shocks me to find that some of us are shy. With the Pure assholes I can understand, but not among our own kind. We're the only ones who understand what it's like to be cast aside for our differences. Judging anyone for who they are would only make us hypocrites.

I walk out back, assessing the scene and finding three angels snuggled together amidst a pile of pillows. Two guys take turns kissing the girl and then each other, oblivious to the onlookers. Or maybe they get off on it. Who the fuck am I to judge?

I wonder what Hayliel will think of this party, and if she'll partake in the festivities or prefer to watch. *And why do I hope she'll only have eyes for me?*

The front door opens just as I come back inside. Hayliel walks in, accompanied by Dina. She and I haven't interacted much since before the summer, but she was pretty wild last year, if my memory serves.

"Zeke!" Dina shouts over the music. "I haven't missed it yet, have I?"

I chuckle, pulling her in for a hug and shaking my head. I forgot how much fun she'd had at our end-of-term party last year. "Nah, things are just getting started."

"Thank fuck. Best parties ever, dude, I swear. If you're feeling adventurous later, Hayles, come out back. But don't wait too long or you'll miss all the fun." She shoots us a wink before taking off outside.

"Do I even want to know?" Hayliel asks, a smile tugging the corner of her lips.

"I guess it all depends on where your tastes lie. We've got some time to figure it out though. Come on." I gesture for her to follow me into the lounge area where neon paint is laid out in various colors.

"How attached are you to these clothes?" I ask, fingering the bottom of her top. The heat of her bare skin brands me, yet I can't seem to pull away.

She bites her lip, looking both confused and intrigued by my question. "Not even a little."

"Good." I pick up the yellow paint and a brush, then draw a sun on each of her cheeks. After dunking the brush back in the pot, I flick it toward her shirt, leaving little dots of paint along her clothes. I do the same with each of the colors until she's the prettiest rainbow I've ever seen.

"Looking good, *Hayles*," I tell her, repeating Dina's nickname.

"Thank you, thank you." She spins once, then stops, looking me up and down. "Hold up. Why aren't you covered in paint? And don't you dare give me some lame-ass bullshit about *house leaders needing to set an example*, because Dina told me you planned this thing." She picks up the brush I just laid down and eyes me critically.

"Maybe I was just waiting for you. Would you like the honors?"

"To bedazzle the house leader? I thought you'd never ask. Now ... How attached are you to these clothes?" she mimics, laughing and walking around me as I stand in the center of the room.

Instead of answering, I grab my shirt with one hand and pull it off entirely. Her eyes damn near bug out of their sockets, and it hits me then just how much I enjoy surprising her.

"Do your worst."

After studying my bare torso for longer than necessary — not that I mind — she dips her brush into the pot of neon-blue paint. "Close your eyes, bigshot."

I do as I'm told, grinning as the soft stroke of the brush hits my flesh. She's gentle, but there's a confidence in whatever artwork she's chosen to design. In this moment, I want nothing but to be her canvas.

With my eyes shut, visions of her dance through my mind. Does she stick out her tongue in concentration? Or perhaps she bites her lip instead. It takes everything inside me not to peek.

Her brush trails lower, down over my abs and almost touches the waistband of my jeans. *By the Archangels.* The need to strip us out of our clothes and fuck her into tomorrow overwhelms me. With all this paint, I bet we'd make a damn fine picture.

Her warm hand cups my stubble-lined cheek as the brush moves up toward my neck in a swirling motion, and I've never been more eager to gaze into a mirror in my life. She controls my head, tilting it this way and that as she paints my jaw and cheek. With our difference in height, it's surprising how steady her hand is.

"Alright. That should do it."

I open my eyes, peering down at the masterpiece which now lives on my chest and stomach. A large pair of multicolored wings covers most of my torso. There's a trail of loose feathers floating along my collarbone and up to my face.

"Holy shit," I breathe, walking toward the mirror on the far side of the wall. As the black lights flicker, the wings on my chest seem to flutter as if come to life.

"I was obsessed with wings as a kid. So much so that there wasn't a single bare spot on the wall in any room. My parents never seemed to mind the thousand vibrant wing drawings. They made sure I had paint or crayons whenever I ran out." She ducks her chin, looking away to focus on painting her hand.

I can't decipher the vulnerability on her face. Whatever she just revealed, I don't think I've fully grasped it yet. Instead of pressing the topic, I change the subject. "Once the others see this, you'll probably end up volun-told to paint everyone next year. I hope you're prepared for that."

"Maybe ..." she replies, distracted, "But I'm not done yet."

From the mirror, I see her approach me from behind and slap a paint-covered hand on my ass before pulling away. I turn to find a wicked smile playing on her lips, one that has my cock hardening in an instant.

"Oh, it's like that, is it?" I rush toward the table, pouring paint directly onto my palm before turning around.

She squeals, darting sideways to avoid me, but I'm too fast. *You won't get away from me that easily, hummingbird.* My hand lands on her ass, smearing paint until it's more of a blob than a print.

We both race back to the table, trying to get as much color on our palms as possible before attacking each other once more. Hayliel might not be as fast as me, but her constant wiggling makes it near impossible to leave a good mark anywhere.

Just then, her hand lands on my other ass cheek and she shouts a triumphant *yes* while fist pumping in the air.

I can only stare at the ethereal creature in front of me, completely caught up in her colorful, paint-covered self, when an idea sparks in my mind.

Her eyes widen as a mischievous smile spreads across my face. Using the paint from my hands, I cover my lips with it and lunge for her. Her shriek turns into laughter as I pull her close, tickling my hands up her body until I reach her neck and push the brown curls off her shoulder.

I lean in close, drawing my nose down the curve of her neck and placing a paint-covered kiss there. Sound seems to melt away until all I can hear is her sharp intake of breath and the pounding of my heart.

The scent of paint blends with honey and sugar in an intoxicating mixture that I'm not sure I'll ever forget.

I pull back, meeting her hungry gaze. Ever since our first meeting, I haven't been able to stop thinking about her. There's something about this Fallen angel who seems both shy and bold all at once that captures my attention.

"Ezekiel," she whispers, still clutching my shoulders.

I'm desperate to kiss her, to mark her body with mine until everyone knows that she's off limits.

My dick throbs in time with my heart as I tilt my head down to kiss her.

"Hayles!" Dina's voice echoes from somewhere close by, breaking the spell wound around us.

Hayliel jolts back, trying to put distance between us, but no amount of air freshener can cover up the lust and desire hanging in the air.

"There you are!" Dina looks between us, her gaze skimming over our paint-coated bodies before she chuckles. "Thanks for getting her ready, Zeke. Come on, girl, you're missing all the action."

Before I can muster up even a single word, Dina tugs Hayliel away from me.

It doesn't matter that we'd just been interrupted. The overwhelming need I have to claim her as mine eats into me, and I already know that I won't be able to stay away from her.

Taking a deep breath, I head outside, not bothering to clean the paint from my lips. I want people to see what I've done. I want them to know I had her, if only for a short time.

The mood outside is more rave than party. A makeshift DJ has set up on the back deck. Lamps that give off ultraviolet light have been dragged about to form a sort of dance floor where half the Fallen students gyrate to the beat and let their inhibitions free, while the other half watches the trio from earlier.

Almost immediately, my eyes are drawn to where Hayliel sits with Dina, utterly enraptured by the threesome currently in full swing on the cushions. As if sensing my gaze, her eyes flick to mine.

By all the Archangels, she's absolutely stunning.

She stands and whispers something to her friend before walking toward me. The kiss I'd placed on her neck glows beneath the UV light, and it's all I can do not to bend her over and claim her here. Not that the other students would mind, but I haven't gotten a good enough read on Hayliel yet to know what she'd think about an audience.

After what feels like an eternity, she finally reaches my position near the sloping hillside beyond the space cleared for dancing. I hadn't realized I'd come this way until now, not fully sure why I had, but nothing seems to make sense when she's near me.

"Hi," she says breathlessly.

At the sound of her voice, something inside of me snaps. I step forward, grabbing her face with my hands and crushing our lips together. She gasps, opening her mouth for me to explore and it only takes a second before she kisses me back.

Sensations roll through me, and it's as if I've stepped into the eye of a storm. Around us, the tempest rages on. Students dance and fuck while music streams from the speakers, but in this spot we're safe. With her, there's only feeling — this urgency to stake my claim and show her just how badly I want her.

Her body presses into mine, molding perfectly into the contours of my own, and I know the exact moment that she notices my erection. At this point, it's fucking hard to miss.

Her hands roam over me with fervent movements, pulling me closer still, like there's far too much distance between us. She slips her fingertips beneath the waistband of my pants, and I damn near explode.

With a strength I didn't know I had, I pull away from her. "What's wrong?"

"Not a damn thing," I reply, allowing my wings to burst free behind me. She gasps, taken by surprise, but I only chuckle before sweeping her off her feet. "Hold on, hummingbird."

With a strong flap of my wings, we're in the air and heading toward the eighth floor. Could I have let her fly on her own?

Absolutely. But I'd rather feel the heat of her body pressed against mine instead.

Tomorrow will be the start of rigorous training and classes, but tonight ... Tonight we don't need to hold back.

5

HAYLIEL

I'm not new to flying, but it's never given me this rush before. In Ezekiel's arms, I feel exhilarated as we hover over the rest of the school. There's something inherently different about holding on to someone else for dear life while soaring through the air. Deep down, I know my wings are there if I need them, but something in the pit of my gut tells me I'm safe.

It's an odd thing to put such faith in someone I've only just met, but with Ezekiel it just feels *right*. Like his soul is already so twisted up with mine that we'll never get them untangled. Why would I even want to?

As we near his balcony, I look back at his massive wings and trail my fingers toward where they join with his shoulders. The shiver that goes through his body is so unmistakable that I can't help but giggle.

When I decided to enroll at this school, I never would have imagined myself sneaking off with someone on my second night here, yet I can't find a single ounce of regret for what we're about to do. This is my chance at a new life. It's about time I take risks, and I can't think of a better way to celebrate than with this dark and delicious angel.

I press a kiss to his throat, trailing my tongue up the side and lightly nipping at his ear.

"Hayliel," he growls. "Keep it up, and I'll fuck you right here in the sky so the entire school will hear your screams as you come for me."

Holy fucking shit. His words are utterly sinful and, for whatever reason, I'm not against the idea of him fucking my brains out above the school population.

Unfortunately for me, though, we land on his balcony, but instead of letting me down, he shifts me in his arms and presses me against the door. I can feel every inch of him as he grinds against me while kissing me deeply. With his wings still spread out behind him, it's like our own piece of paradise.

I kiss him back, running my hands along his feathers and causing him to groan. I want to make him fall apart. To destroy him completely, only to help put the pieces back together again.

"If I don't get you inside this very moment, I swear I'll devour you right here." He lowers me slowly to the ground and backs away to press a wing tip to the little box beside the door. A soft click sounds before he grabs my hand and tugs me inside.

I don't get even a moment to look around before his hands are on me, pressing me against him and causing my stomach to tighten. Who the fuck cares what his room looks like, anyway? I'm way more fucking interested to see what the rest of *him* looks like beneath those clothes.

I let my gaze wander over his body. The paint on his chest no longer glows without the blacklight, but I can still see the colorful wings I'd painted there. I can also see the massive bulge in his pants that has my heart rate skyrocketing.

He dips his head, grazing his teeth against my neck and trailing a hand over my body until shivers dance along my skin. I don't want foreplay tonight. What I want is for him to devour me like he promised. I need him to make me scream until I lose my voice.

He cups my cheek, and I can't help but lean in to the caress of his thumb over my bottom lip.

"Last chance to back out, Hayliel. Once I get a taste of you, I don't think I'll ever be able to stop." His words crash over me, drowning me in their truth. This thing between us is unlike anything I've experienced before, and I would rather die than stop.

"I need you." The words come out whimpered and desperate, but I can't focus on how embarrassed I'd normally feel because he growls and tosses me onto the bed.

I sit on my knees, watching this glorious angel stride toward me with a wicked gleam in his green eyes. Slowly, piece by fucking piece, he takes off my clothes. There's something so sensual about another person undressing you, and I know he'll find out soon just how hot I am for him.

When I stand in only my panties and bra, he trails a finger up the wet fabric of my underwear. "So wet for me already," he says, then lowers his head and kisses me through the fabric.

I moan, surprised by the sudden move, but it only proves to spur me on further. As he continues, I twine my fingers through his dark hair, desperate to feel him on my bare flesh. Finally, he pulls away, tearing the last shred of my clothes off.

For a moment, all he does is stare. I try not to let the self-conscious thoughts in, but even I know it's futile. Not with this half-naked muscled god kneeling before me.

He stands, grabbing my legs before pulling me to the edge of the bed and dropping to his knees. "Spread those pretty legs for me."

And that's it. This is how I die. With the way he's talking, I know without a single doubt that I'll be leaving a goddamn snail trail on his bed. And he's barely even touched me!

I sit up on my elbows, watching as he nips and kisses my thighs, his five o'clock shadow scratching against my oversensitive flesh. But he never once touches me where I want him to the most.

"Ezekiel …" I whine. I'm past the point of caring how I sound. So what if I'm a needy bitch? Nothing matters except more of this. Of him.

"Call me Zeke. Now tell me what you want, hummingbird," he replies, his voice a deep timber. But he bloody well knows what I want and is actively avoiding it. The fucker.

I stay quiet, hoping he'll get the hint as I raise my hips and try to direct him, but he only moves aside. Sometimes he gets close, the edge of his lips touching my clit slightly and by the smirk on his stupidly handsome face when he pulls back, I know he's doing it on purpose.

With a groan, I give in. "I want your mouth on me."

"Here?" He presses a kiss to the inside of my knee.

I roll my eyes. "No."

"How about here?" He trails his tongue a little higher, his face close to my core.

"No." I'm seconds away from flipping us over and sitting on his gorgeous goddamn face when he hovers over my pussy.

"And here?" His breath is hot against me, causing a shiver to run down my spine. Before I can answer, he closes the distance.

"Yes!" I moan, tossing my head back as he licks and sucks the very soul from my body. My pussy pulses with a longing to be filled, but I don't want him to pull away. He picks up his pace, my orgasm building rapidly with each passing second. Somehow he knows my body already, can sense that I'm so fucking close, but instead of giving me what I need, he slows down.

"You liked the idea of me fucking you in the sky, didn't you?"

Damn. How can he read me so easily?

"Don't even try to deny it. I felt your body react when I made my threat and, by all the Archangels, Hayliel, I almost fucked you among the clouds. Answer me truthfully and you'll have your orgasm."

I bite my lip and contemplate just rolling over to get myself off or even lying to get what I crave, but I'm not that stupid. The truth for an orgasm. That I can do. *It's not like he's asking me to unfurl my wings.*

"Of course I fucking liked it. And maybe someday I'll let you, but I swear, Zeke, if you don't—"

His eyes darken a split second before he lowers his mouth to me again. If I thought he had skill earlier, it's nothing compared to this. I've been hovering on the brink of release for far too long, and finally, it comes crashing down around me.

My legs try to close as he continues his onslaught, but his massive shoulders get in the way. It's both torture and ecstasy all at once, and it's not long before another orgasm coils through me.

When my release subsides, I'm as limp as a wet fucking noodle. Zeke stands, unbuttoning his jeans and pulling them down. The moment I see his thick erection burst free, I perk up. Like the energizer bunny, I'm ready to go again, and I need him inside me.

I flip on the bed, crawling toward his naked form with my mouth practically salivating. What in the fuck is going on with me today? I have never, not once in my entire existence, been so desperate to suck a dick. Not that I don't enjoy it — or at least I think I would, if the few people I'd fooled around with weren't total asshats — but this is different. The need to taste him consumes me.

He doesn't make a move, only watching as I reach out to grip his cock. My fingers wrap around his base, and I dip forward to lick the bead of pre-cum off the tip. But he doesn't let me get any further.

A growl reverberates deep in his chest as he flips me over until I'm on all fours in front of him. He trails his cock up and down my slick entrance once, twice, then a third time.

"Zeke, please." I'm fully prepared to beg again, but he must be just as impatient as I am because he thrusts forward, sheathing himself to the hilt.

My mouth falls open as he plants himself within me, his thick cock stretching me and making my inner walls flutter around him.

"Look at how well you take me, baby." Slowly pulling back, he stares at his cock as it disappears inside of me once more. "So. Fucking. Perfect." He thrusts inside of me with unhurried strokes, torturing me.

I meet his every movement, slamming him into me and hoping he'll get the hint. These situations are always so strange. Do I speak up or just keep quiet? I don't want him to think I'm criticizing his skill, not when all I want is for him to fuck my brains out.

Just as I muster up the nerve to say something, he chuckles. "If you want rough, hummingbird, all you have to do is ask."

I peer behind me, our eyes locking. "I don't want to make love, Zeke. You promised me screams."

His grip tightens around my hips as the smile spreads on his face, and suddenly the once-slow movements turn into something else. It's like night and day. I'm nothing but an island caught in the storm of his thrusts as they crash into me.

My release builds higher and higher until I'm sure I'll have bruises tomorrow. I hope I do. I want to ache with the reminder of tonight and see the proof of his touch on my skin.

Without warning, he shifts, leaning back slightly and hitting a spot so deep inside of me that I shatter instantly, a scream ripping from my throat as my pleasure explodes.

"What was that, baby? You want more?" he asks, reaching around to play with my clit.

My arms give out and I fall forward, the side of my face pressed into his sheets, but he doesn't stop. Blinding pleasure enfolds me, overloading my flesh with so much sensation that it's almost painful.

"That's it. Give me one more." His voice shakes as he teeters on the edge of control.

As if by his command alone, I fall once more into ecstasy. My pussy convulses around him as I scream his name, forcing him to come too. He groans, pumping his cock inside of me and riding out our orgasms for as long as possible until I'm nothing but a pile of mush.

I can't move, my limbs spent and sated beyond anything I've ever experienced. With his arms wrapped around my waist, I close my eyes and drift off to sleep.

Did I sneak out of his room like a burglar? Okay, yes. But I'm not willing to start my first day of classes with the walk of shame. That doesn't quite excuse why I took his shirt, but that's beside the point.

I'd woken up in Zeke's bed, completely lost to where I was or how I'd gotten there, but it didn't take long for the memories to surface. After I'd fallen asleep, he must have cleaned me up, because the mess I'd expected to find between my legs wasn't there. At least I didn't have to worry about getting pregnant. It isn't just a game of chance with angels. The females of our kind choose if and when we're ready, opening our bodies to the possibility of fertility, and I kept that shit locked down.

I hadn't stayed long enough to let the kindness of his aftercare sink in, and instead I took off down the flight of stairs to my room on the seventh floor.

Thankfully, no one witnessed me leaving the house leader's floor in the middle of the night. I'll have enough on my plate today without fielding questions about that. Not that it would have changed anything. Fucking Zeke had been more than worth it, and I want to do it again. *Just get through the day, Hayles. Then you can worry about screwing your brains out.*

My slate pings, breaking me from the pleasure-induced fog I'm in and reminding me just how important today is. *And how fucking late I am.*

I was supposed to grab breakfast with Dina, but I overslept. By the missed messages, it's clear she'd banged on my door for a good ten minutes before sending a barrage of private messages. None of which woke me up.

I can't help it that these beds are as soft and squishy as cotton candy. Mix that with bone-deep satisfaction, and it's a wonder I woke up at all.

Not only have I missed breakfast, but I'm very close to showing up late to my first class. I take a detour to grab a croissant from the cafeteria — because I'd rather be late than hangry — and rush to class.

Wingology. The name alone makes me want to avoid it at all costs. Flashes of "abomination" and "freak" whisper through my mind. I don't want to expose myself yet. Not when I'm having so much fun just being normal, but luck doesn't appear to be on my side today. Or any day, really.

I arrive at the arena and quickly realize everyone else is already sitting on the bleachers listening to the teacher. Fuck. *Can today get any worse? Actually, no. I take that back. Nope. I'm not jinxing it.*

I hadn't bothered to don my uniform before coming, choosing to put on the outfit provided by the school for all flight-related classes. Skintight leggings paired with a racerback top, both of which sport the school's emblem — the letters SCU intertwined together. After tossing everything into a locker, I rush to the back of the students, hoping to arrive unnoticed.

For a moment, it seems as if I've managed the impossible. Until the teacher calls my name.

"Here!" I call back, hoping maybe he's only taking attendance. *Why the hell haven't I been paying attention?*

"Do you plan to show up late for all classes, or is it only the morning ones you have trouble with?" His bushy eyebrows pull down over his eyes as he frowns.

Most of the students chuckle, causing my face to flush hot.

"No, Professor. It won't happen again," I reply, trying to keep my voice steady. Shit. What was this professor's name again? Ulrich or Uriah ... fuck. *You've got to pay attention!*

"We'll see. Because of your tardiness, you've just volunteered yourself to go first. Please step forward."

My stomach falls all the way to the Underworld. This can't be happening, can it? I pinch my arm, hoping I'll wake up beside Zeke and realize this is all just a terrible nightmare. But nope. This is real.

As I stand in front of the class full of Pure and Fallen angels, all I want to do is disappear. A very tiny part of me — the hopeful, optimistic part — keeps repeating that maybe I won't need to show my wings. Maybe all I need to do is answer some questions and put this all behind me. *Or maybe my life's a hot damn mess and I'm about to ruin any shot at normalcy I hope to have.*

"As I was saying," the professor continues, running a hand through his mousy brown hair, "in this class we will learn the basics of our greatest asset. Our wings. Not only do they provide us with a quick getaway option in times of need, but they can also serve as a shield or a weapon."

Hope grows inside of me as he speaks. I can do this. I know countless facts about wings and feathers. Hell, it's always fascinated me because I'm different. I'll show off my knowledge and then sit the fuck down and never be late to this class again.

"Hayliel, please open your wings for the class."

"Erm ... Say what now?"

The class chuckles again, but the embarrassment I expect to feel doesn't come. How can I feel embarrassed when my fight-or-flight response begs me to run? Every atom in my body screams to leave, to make an excuse, anything to let me keep my secret a little longer.

Faking my death sounds damn good right about now.

"Professor Uriel, I believe Hayliel needs you to say it in fewer words in order for her to understand," a flat-faced angel says, causing the rest of the class to burst out laughing.

"Quiet," the professor demands. "Today's lesson is on the individuality of our wings. We all have them, but that does not mean each one is the same. Our focus today will be on comparing the difference between things such as width, angle, length, and color to see if we can find any similarities. Each of you will get the chance to come up and reveal them to your classmates before we take a closer look."

I almost laugh. Not because what he's saying is funny, but because he truly picked the worst topic for class if he wanted me to go first. "Professor, I'd really rather not have everyone staring at my wings ..."

"If you are uncomfortable now, Miss Hayliel, then I suggest you pack your bags and leave. Otherwise, show us your wings so we can move on."

I can't swallow past the lump in my throat. Leaving isn't an option for me. Not when I have absolutely nothing outside of this school. All I ever fucking wanted was to be normal. To have friends who like me for who I am and don't avoid me because I'm different. But even I'm not that stupid. I can either stay and be the school's freak show or leave and end up a lonely freak instead. At least here I'm closer to finding out what having gray wings even means.

I take a deep breath, then center myself as I close my eyes. Eventually I'll find people who can see past my quirks, but if I continue to run from who I am, then I never will. How can I expect others to accept me if I don't even accept myself?

At my command, the wings burst free from my back, and I open my eyes amidst a flurry of shocked gasps. Everyone stares, their faces a mixture of shock and disbelief. Some even look horrified, as if I just whipped out my vagina and started using it to bash cymbals together.

Whispers grow louder throughout the arena as everyone continues to gape, and my confidence falters. *Well, there goes my chance at a normal school year.*

Looking at the ground, I tuck my wings in against my side and wish to be anywhere but here.

"Is this a joke to you, Miss Hayliel? Do you think rolling around in ashes and soot before class is a good way to make friends? Dust it off immediately."

Now it's my turn to stare. He can't seriously think I rolled around in the dirt to pull some stupid prank, can he?

"These are my true wings, Professor." I flap them hard, whipping up a breeze to prove it. The ground beneath my feet is dry packed dirt, but I'd flapped hard enough to whip up the loose particles around me. Dust coats my tongue as I breathe through the discomfort of being on display.

As the air settles around us, most of the students are still staring at me wary eyed, and some even have their slates out. I flip them off, infuriated with them for reacting so poorly, even if I'm not surprised.

And, as always, I'm annoyed with myself too. Why do I have to be so fucking different?

"You leave me no choice but to take you to the principal. Students, I'd like you to please continue with the scheduled lesson. I'll be back momentarily." To me he says, "Retrieve your things from the locker and meet me at the main hall." He frees his milky-white wings and points me toward the exit.

I look back at my classmates once more, feeling their eyes on me like a weight. No one smiles or sends me reassuring looks like I'd hoped, so I turn and head back to the locker room.

It's time to find out if I can stay at Silver City University or if I'll be stuck as the lonely freak after all.

6

HAYLIEL

“There has been a grievous slight played on me today, Principal Cael. Not only did Miss Hayliel show up late to my class, but she then attempted to prank me by covering her wings in soot.” Professor Uriel turns to me, his eyes accusing. “You thought I was too stupid to notice, did you? Well, let me tell you—“

“That will be all, Uriel. I have heard your words and will take it from here. Please go back to class,” Principal Cael says, shooting him a soft smile.

With a calculated smirk shot my way, the professor exits the room and leaves me standing, wings out, in front of the man who holds my fate in his hands.

This is it. Expelled on my first day ... That's bound to be a record, right? At least I had a few enjoyable moments while I was here. Those memories might just be my only companions when I leave.

To my surprise, it isn't a lecture that comes out of the principal's mouth. "Before you sit down, Miss Hayliel, do you mind if I inspect your wings?"

"I ... Yes, of course." I'm off balance, unsure if his pleasant demeanor will change once he realizes there is no dirt and I'm truly just an abomination.

How many times have authority figures tricked me in that exact way? A teacher at my old school, the bus driver before that, and even the parents of some students I used to call friends back when I believed in happily ever after. I won't fall for it this time.

Principal Cael stands, and I spread my wings as wide as his office will allow. He circles me, surveying them with a detached interest that makes me want to squirm under his scrutiny.

The scent of apples reaches me from a lit candle burning on his desk. I focus all my attention on the flame, using it to help calm my nerves.

"May I?" he asks, his soft gray eyes assessing me while his hand hovers over my left wing.

I nod, not entirely sure I want him touching them, but at this point I'll do anything to stay here. *Well, maybe not anything.*

My body tenses against the incoming invasion, but he only touches one feather, wiping his finger down its length before checking it for residue. When he finds none, he clucks his tongue and heads back to his seat. Bringing out a notebook, he scribbles several lines down before shutting it and tucking it back into his desk.

"You may put your wings away now, Miss Hayliel, and sit. Thank you for indulging my curiosity."

I follow his direction and sit down on the edge of the seat, clasping my hands in front of me to stop them from shaking. *Why did I think this school would be any different?*

"I'm sorry, Principal Cael," I say, but he cuts me off.

"Sorry for what, exactly? Did you roll around in ash before class with the hopes of pranking your teacher?"

"Well, no." *Though I wish I had.*

"Then I don't see what you need to be sorry for. Aside from being tardy, of course. Rules are there for a reason, Miss Hayliel, and I assure you that reason is not to break them."

"I understand." The words leave a bitter taste in my mouth. I very much don't understand. I can't tell if I'm in trouble, and my anxiety is through the roof just waiting for the other shoe to drop.

"Good. Given the circumstances, it's best not to invite additional trouble, don't you think? I will send a memo to your other teachers so that this doesn't keep happening, but I need you to do your part as well. Show up on time, do your work, and I'm sure your future here at Silver City University will be a bright one."

"Thank you, sir. I'll be on time going forward, I promise." As I say the words, I glance at the clock above his desk and worry that I'm about to make a liar out of myself. *Okay, so maybe I'll be late for one more class.*

"I've already sent a message to your second period teacher, notifying them you'll be late. There is a bathroom outside my office. You may use it to change out of your flying gear."

I look from him to the door, completely dumbfounded by his generosity.

"Thank you again, Principal Cael."

He shoots me a pained glance and clears his throat. As I leave his office, I hear him say, "Don't thank me yet, Miss Hayliel. You still need to get through the day."

I change quickly. Despite having an excuse to be late, I don't want to bring any more attention to myself. *Archangels know I'll have enough of that today as it is.*

Was it truly only last night that I crept out of Zeke's bed? I should have stayed there, wrapped up in his powerful arms. Maybe then things would have been different.

I dig through my bag until I find my slate, still not believing the school gives out the latest model. With an all-you-can-eat meal plan and technology supplied, it's no wonder tuition costs are so high.

My schedule isn't too jam packed, despite my double major — Wingology and History. As with all first-year students, there are some courses we're required to take regardless of our focus, but next year I'll have a bit more freedom to build my class load. There's even a course about the Earth Realm that I hope to take. I may never get to go there, but at least I can read about it.

With my uniform on and my half-empty bag slung over my shoulders, I make my way toward my next class.

Luckily for me, it's in the same building as the principal's office, only on the complete other side of the building. At least the hallways are empty. I can pretend for a little while longer that my life at this school hasn't changed.

I should have known better than to let myself think that. It's almost as bad as saying 'what's the worst that can happen' or 'things can't possibly get any worse.'

Three angels step out from the girls' bathroom, directly blocking my path.

I move off to the side, out of their way, but they follow me until I find myself stuck in the middle of their triangle.

Not one of them looks familiar, so I don't think I've ever spoken to them before, but the way they're acting makes me think I've done something wrong.

"Excuse me," I say, trying to push past them. "I have to get to class."

"Do you hear that, girls? The demon-spawn needs to get to class," the blonde one taunts, her eyes flashing with disgust.

"Demon-spawn," the second girl, a mousy brunette, replies through a chuckle.

"Good one, Seraphina," the third girl replies, her smile cruel.

Well that's a new one. Ouch.

I knew the insults were coming, but then why does it hurt so much? My experience with bullies has taught me they aren't all the same. Some do it to feel better about themselves, but sometimes angels are just vicious for the sake of it. I don't know enough about these girls to know which one they are, so I stay quiet.

"I'm surprised the university is even allowing you to stay. What's stopping you from going full demon on us and killing everyone here? You're a liability, really. Once my father hears about the monstrosity they've let in, it won't be long before you're shipped back to the gutter you crawled out of." Seraphina folds her arms across her chest, a wicked smile playing on her lips, but still I stay silent.

"Do you not speak, demon?"

"Maybe her forked tongue makes her fuck up the words."

It takes everything within me not to lash out. All they want from me is a reaction. It wouldn't matter what words passed my lips because they just don't care. They want me to hurt, and they want to be the ones making it happen.

"No one wants you here," Seraphina says, getting right up in my face. She's taller than my five-foot-two frame and uses every inch to peer down her nose at me. "Now that your little secret is out, no Pure angel would dare sully themselves by being near you, and honestly, I'd be surprised if any of the Fallen would either. You're all alone."

She brushes past me, snapping her fingers so her friends follow along. Without turning back, she says, "Let's go, girls. If we spend any more time with the demon-spawn, her filth might rub off on us."

I stand as still as the stone statues out front, completely un-moving until I can't feel their presence anymore. Only then do I realize I'm holding my breath, my lungs aching for air. I pull in oxygen, my chest heaving and limbs shaking as I try to calm myself. *This is nothing,* I tell myself. *You've been through way worse than this and come out the other side.*

All they have is words.

7

THEO

Two demon attacks since last week.

Instead of keeping informed on the situation, I'm stuck in fucking class. Don't get me wrong, I love school. Knowledge is power, I believe it. The more someone knows, the better equipped they are to handle life. It's the unknown that's scary. We just don't know what we don't know.

But learning about aerodynamics and our history seems like a waste when the future is so fucked. The demons are clearly planning something. Who cares about flying faster when there are angels getting attacked in their homes? That won't protect us from death.

What will focusing on the past do for us when the monsters put their plan into action? It's like the entire city expects us to bury our heads in the sand and act like nothing's wrong. I can't do that.

Professor Castiel sits at his desk, occupied by the paperwork in front of him. I've only got two more classes to get through and then I can give the news my full attention.

Just a little longer.

My slate vibrates in my pocket, and I pull it out despite the likelihood class will start any moment. *Recent Attacks: Demons or Hoax?*

What a fucking joke. My grip tightens on the slate until I can practically feel the metal shifting beneath my fingers. I read a little further down, my chest tightening as I search for any names I might recognize. When I don't find any, I take a deep breath to calm my pounding heart.

The attack might not have been on anyone I know personally, but the location has the hair on my neck standing on end.

A shop near the entertainment district was the scene of a brutal demon attack late last night. A lone Pure angel managed to hold off his assailant and escape. He's currently seeking medical treatment for his wounds while the Guild has opened an investigation to better understand what happened.

Demons haven't ever come this far into Silver City. The Assassins' Guild has always kept them far from civilization, so how are they getting past our defenses? And what is it the demons are after?

My mouth dries as bloody images of death and destruction flash behind my eyes. If they made it to the entertainment district, what's to stop them from coming to SCU?

I stare at my slate for so long the screen turns black and all that's left is my own face gazing back. My brown, curly hair looks like it always does, but today it's even more unruly than usual. I study the rest of my face before finally moving to my best feature: my hazel eyes. But in my reflection, they appear almost empty, like these recent attacks are finally displaying the fact that I'm dead inside. I frown and look away.

The door creaks open suddenly and a short, brunette angel with her face buried in a map rushes in, barely paying attention to where she's going. As she passes the third row of desks, a long-haired boy sticks out his leg. The girl doesn't notice until she trips over his foot, and I watch as she almost collides with the corner of my desk.

I stand, pushing the desk out of the way so that she crashes into me instead. "Look, I know we're damn near invincible, but it really helps if you look where you're going."

With my hands on her arms, I pull back and instantly recognize her as the girl Raphael's become obsessed with. She must be a foot shorter than me, so she has to tilt her head to look up at me. When her eyes meet mine, they're wide pools of blue sapphire. Hidden amongst the blue are flecks of silver and gold, reminding me of rare granite, and I can't tear myself away.

We're so close that the heat of her body seeps into mine, and the sugar-sweet scent of honey fills my nose.

"Shit, sorry. I got lost earlier and then couldn't find the class details ... Today is just not my day." Seeming to collect herself, she steps back and tucks a stray lock of dark hair from her face.

"Why don't you sit here," I offer, pulling out the empty seat beside me. I'd already stopped four angels from sitting there, but none of them were her. "We can compare schedules and I'd be happy to help you get around."

Raphael will be so jealous when he learns who I spent an entire hour of class with. Neither of us have seen much of her today, though I know he'd been hoping to share at least a few classes with her, especially after what happened this morning.

"I'd love that, actually. Thank you," she says tentatively, shifting her gaze between the staring students and me like I'll take back my offer any second. When I don't, she places her belongings on the desk beside mine and takes the seat I offer.

"I'm Theo. And you must be the infamous Hayliel. Quite the first day, huh?"

A pretty blush spreads across her face as she drops her eyes, and I immediately kick myself. Fuck. It isn't any secret that she's been getting picked on since revealing herself this morning, so why the fuck had I felt it necessary to bring it up?

She shoots me a sad smile as she stands and picks her be-longings up. "I'll understand if you don't want to associate with me anymore. No hard feelings."

"What? No. I'm sorry, that was a stupid thing to say," I reply, placing my hand on her arm to stop her. A jolt of electricity thrums through me with the contact, and I almost lose my train of thought. "Look, I don't really care what color your wings are, and I'll be the first to admit that my research-focused brain wants to know more about what it means, but I would never treat you like shit because of it. And neither should anyone else."

Her gaze meets mine, holding for an entire minute before she sits back down. "That would make you the first, I think. And trust me, I want to know why I have these damn gray wings just as much as anyone, but I'm just tired of talking about it today. So can we just pretend I'm normal for now? Please?"

My heart practically tears in two at the defeat in her voice, and I try to imagine what her life must be like. I might have had to live with the pain of my own mistakes, but hers was unavoidable. The color of her wings is out of anyone's control, but it doesn't stop others from being assholes about it.

Before I can respond, the professor stands from his desk at the front of the class. "Welcome to your first history lecture. I'm Professor Castiel. In this class, we'll focus on delving into the past so that we might learn the mistakes of our forefathers and perhaps gain the skills needed to prevent them. This class will require regular reading on your own time, all of which will be available on your slate. Before I send over the first lesson, I'd like to see what you already know. I'll presume you know the basic types of angels since you're all in my university class, but what about in the past?"

I raise my hand, confident in my answer. "Depending how far back we're going, we'd also have the Cherub, Seraphim, and Demons. Technically, the latter aren't angels anymore, but if history is to be believed, they were at one point."

"Very good, Theo," Professor Castiel says with a smile. "Since the dawn of time, our kind have evolved and grown. Demons, while not angels, still exist and plague us. But the only of our kind left in existence are the Pure, Fallen, and the Archangels who rule Silver City. Please look at your slates and answer the questions there as best you can. This will help me determine the content for our class."

I make my way through the questions, not surprised to find I know most of the answers already, when a hand rests lightly on my arm. I turn to Hayliel, finding she's finished answering her questions too.

"Something tells me you're bunked in the Knowledge house. I bet your parents must have had their hands full." She chuckles, seeming at ease with me for the first time.

Before I can reply, a guy with dirty-blonde hair sitting a few rows in front of us speaks up. "Professor, I think we forgot a species. Gray wings aren't exactly Pure or Fallen, and from what I've heard, she doesn't have extra wings like the Archangels. So how do we know she's not an unturned demon?"

The class laughs, and I watch the easy smile melt from Hayliel's face. Anger erupts from me, and all I want to do is put whoever said that in their place. I'm not one for drama and I avoid most people at all costs, but I can't just stand by while these piece-of-shit angels pick on Hayliel for something beyond her control. She's still one of us, and we shouldn't turn on our own. I stand forcefully, the legs of my chair scraping across the floor. I'm ready to teach this angel a lesson, but the professor beats me to it.

"Some believe we also have the subspecies of idiot, Cadriel, and it appears you may have that gene." The class turns silent as Professor Castiel pulls a slip of paper from his drawer, signs it, and walks it over to a guy in the middle of class. I immediately recognize him as the angel who tripped Hayliel earlier.

"You can't talk to me like that, Professor!" Cadriel says, his face turning red.

"I most certainly can. I'd like to remind all students that my class — and indeed the university — holds zero tolerance for bullying. Anyone caught doing so will receive an immediate warning and after two strikes, I will personally ensure expulsion. Have I made myself clear?"

Silence falls, and after a beat, Professor Castiel claps his hands. "Good. Back to your tests now."

I sit back down, scooting closer to Hayliel. "Don't worry about them. Not all of us are idiots." I send her a reassuring smile, but her frown doesn't lift. Students stare at her, their tests forgotten while they gaze at the unusual angel beside me.

"I know he's just trying to help, but I think forcing detention and threatening expulsion on these assholes will only make it worse," she whispers, defeated. "Thank you, though, for whatever it is you were going to do."

"Friends don't let friends deal with assholes alone," I tell her, knocking my shoulder into hers.

Professor Castiel makes his way through the aisles, checking on students' progress and assisting where needed. When he approaches our table, he gives us a wide, genuine smile. "Hayliel, Theo, I see you've both completed your papers. Very good, as expected. Once I check your answers, I'll likely have some extra credit assignments for you both in the coming weeks, should you be interested. Let me know."

He walks away, leaving us both puzzled. *But it's not like I can turn down extra credit. I might need all the help I can get.*

I look around the class, memorizing the faces of those too stupid to look away. There's something about Hayliel that makes my heart pound and the blood rush beneath my skin. I'll protect her in any way that I can, and I have a feeling Raphael will do the same.

"Give me your slate," I demand, holding out my hand.

She hesitates but passes it to me anyway, and I program my contact details into it. "There. Send me your schedule and we can compare classes. If you ever need an escape or just a friend, I'll be there."

Her eyes glisten, some emotion flashing there that I can't quite read. It's clear that my offer isn't one she receives often. For whatever reason, I feel tethered to her, and I know from experience just how rare those relationships can be.

I won't let her handle this alone. I can't.

8

HAYLIEL

It turns out that Theo and I don't share as many classes together as I hoped, but I'm grateful for the few we do share. It was nice to have someone to talk to, especially after what that Cadriel guy said in front of the entire class. *News of your wings is bound to blow over soon, Hayles.*

After comparing our schedules, it's only Theo and I left in class. We pack up our things, both of us excited to only have one class standing in the way of our freedom, but as we head toward the door, Professor Castiel calls out to us.

"Miss Hayliel, I'd like a word if you don't mind."

Theo shoots me a questioning glance, but I only smile and nod. It's nice of him to worry, but Professor Castiel has been nothing but kind to me so far and, for whatever reason, I trust him.

Taking my answer, he nods and waves before taking off while I turn around to see what else this day might bring.

"How are things going?" the professor asks me, sitting on the edge of his desk. "I hope what I witnessed in class hasn't been happening all day ..."

I swallow, unsure what to say. I could be honest and tell him that comments like that have been almost constant, but what's the point? He can't throw everyone in detention, and the last thing I want to do is put a target on his back. *Or an even bigger one on mine.*

"No, no, that was the first. I appreciate what you were trying to do, Professor. Thank you for being so kind to me."

He watches me for a moment before responding, and I wonder if he can see through the lie. "Being rude has far more cost on the soul than being kind, my dear. I do hope you'll come to me if something like that happens again."

"I will." I'm stunned by his offer, and a little skeptical. Aside from Dina, who already knew my secret, that's two angels who have offered me kindness despite the big wing reveal. What are their motives for being so kind? Surely they have one. *Everyone else does.*

"You best get going then, child. Your next class will start soon."

I thank him again on my way out, pulling out the map to find my next class. As much as I want to hide away and avoid my lessons, I need to keep my grades up to maintain my scholarship. The principal made it clear that showing up on time played a big part in my continued success here, and that's exactly what I intend to do.

As I head toward my next class, the first one taught in the Tower, I can't help but think about Theo. How is it that a total stranger could be so kind to me? I have a firm target on my back and it's like he doesn't care, but why? I'm the campus weirdo. As grateful as I am for his gift, I can't help but wonder what it is he gets out of it.

I look up and realize I'm standing in the doorway of my next class. Despite staying late to talk to Professor Castiel and the seemingly endless number of stairs I had to climb, I've gotten here in record time. The room is empty, so I make my way toward the back and slump into a seat in the last row, as far away from anyone as I can get.

Taking out my slate, I open a new document and write *Angelic Powers* at the top. Regardless of the shitty day I've had, I can't stop the jittery feeling of excitement that comes when I think about using my powers. My parents couldn't attend a university like this one and don't have as much control over their powers as the Pure angels do, so I'm excited to see what I can master. Then, maybe I can teach my parents what I learn.

A few students enter the class, whispering loudly about the mutant angel before taking their seats in the middle of the room. I really should be used to it by now, but every comment hurts more than the last.

The teacher enters the room next, followed by Raphael. My heart skips a beat as I wait for him to notice me. I hold my breath, waiting to see what he'll do.

Part of me doesn't want to know. If he rejects me now after our meeting in the cafeteria, I'm not sure I'll be able to handle it.

But it turns out I have nothing to worry about. I've been so prepared for rejection that I can barely believe his reaction. His icy-blue eyes light up when he sees me, and he makes a beeline in my direction before falling into the empty seat next to me.

"I was hoping you'd be in this class. I heard the professor is obsessed with full-term partners, so you're about to be stuck with me for a while, sunshine." He smiles, nudging into me, and I can't help but laugh as the tension leaves my body.

It's like I've just woken from an icy slumber and my brain is finally thawing. His demeanor hasn't changed in the slightest, which makes me think maybe he hasn't heard the news.

"I wasn't sure you'd still talk to me. Most angels stay away for fear of catching my disease."

He shifts his entire body toward me, and his face turns serious. "Well, those angels are idiots. We can't get diseases, everyone knows that." A smile spreads across his lips once more as he says, "Besides, they can fuck off for all I care. It only means I get you to myself."

"Wow, you must have eaten well before class. That's some top-tier charm you've got today."

The teacher shuts the door before returning to the front of the class, her straight, auburn hair swaying behind her when she turns to address us. "I'm Professor Isidora, and I'll be teaching you all about the many angelic powers we possess. As you know, we are gifted with several abilities, but that doesn't mean each of you will master all of them. In my experience, those angels are few and far between. Regardless, we will learn the basic fundamentals of each. As you progress through this class, we'll determine where your strengths and weaknesses lie and develop a specific syllabus for each of you. The student beside you will be your partner for the entire term. I implore you to get to know them, as the bond you form will help you succeed in this class."

"Professor Isidora, I'd like to pick my own partner."

"Yes, I'm sure many of you would like to, but that is not how I do things. For now, I want you to practice telepathy with your partners and then write a five-hundred-word report on the process. You may begin."

A notification pops up on my slate with a link to the list of telepathy instructions. I read through them briefly while Raphael does the same, but I can't focus on the words. *Someone's watching me.*

Seraphina glares at me from her seat in the middle of class. *Great. Just great.*

It doesn't take a genius to guess that I've stepped on her toes where Raphael is concerned, even though I've done nothing but be friendly toward him and it was *him* going out of his way to speak with me. I wonder if it was him she was referring to earlier when she gave me the 'no Pure would ever want you' speech. *Does Raphael know?*

"Have you done this before?" Raphael asks, jerking me from my thoughts.

My cheeks flame, but I try to shake off the embarrassment. I can't be the only angel at this school coming from an under-privileged family. "Both of my parents are Fallen, so I have very little experience with abilities. Have you?"

He nods. "My older brother and I don't really get along. In the eyes of my parents he could do no wrong, even though he was constantly setting me up to get in trouble. My friend and I practiced for months until we perfected telepathy as a way to escape."

For the first time since I met Raphael, I see through the cheer-ful optimism. This is a man who's fought to be seen. Whatever he'd gone through with his family, I'm glad to know he had someone to rely on. And if I'm honest, I'm glad he hasn't shut me out.

"Alright, how do we do this? The notes just say to *open your mind and speak your truth,* but honestly, that sounds like a crock of shit."

He laughs, the sound so cheerful I can't help but smile too. "We both have to let down our mental shields. It's easier when there's trust involved. Do you trust me, sunshine?"

My answer should be no, yet when I actually think about it, I realize I do. I give a tentative nod, which only causes his lips to tilt upward.

"Good." He grabs hold of my chair and turns it to face him. For a moment, I'm trapped, held captive by his nearness. A bomb could go off and I doubt I'd even notice.

Our knees touch, only the fabric of our school uniforms between us, and my insides thrum with anticipation. But I can't really be considering this, can I? I woke up beside another angel this morning before I high-tailed it out of there, for fuck's sake. Now is so not the time to fantasize about anything with anyone.

"All you need to do is stare into my eyes and focus on our connection. Ready?" he asks, his smile wicked.

It's as if a pair of angels take flight within my belly, making me feel almost giddy, but I nod and do as he asks. At first there's nothing, only the arctic blue of his eyes as they bore into mine. Then I hear it. *You light up any room you enter, do you know that?*

I grin, my heart pounding, and a second later—

Good. Now you try. Tell me how dashing I look.

A huff of laughter escapes me as I try to press the words into his mind, but it doesn't work. Do I just think about them while we're connected? What if I shoot them to the wrong person and accidentally tell someone else how attractive they are? Fuck. I have no clue what I'm doing.

Breathe. His voice is back in my mind, and I follow his orders. *Think the words in my direction, and if you're worried, just call me an asshole and then it won't matter who gets it.*

I try multiple times, failing at every turn until I'm beyond frustrated. When I attempt it again, I practically shout the word *asshole* and, to my surprise, his eyes flash triumphantly.

You did it! Somehow his voice sounds the same inside my head — a cheerful, almost familiar tone with his excitement coming across loud and clear — and I realize in this moment just how much I like Raphael. He's a refreshing mix of funny and happy, and when he mentioned his brother I saw a flash of pain floating beneath the surface that even now I want to sooth. Like a kindred spirit, he sucks me in.

He holds up his hand, offering me a high five. When our hands meet, he doesn't let go. For a second, all he does is trail his thumb across the back of my hand, causing shivers to race up my spine.

"Good. Physical contact will help," he says, before he pulls our joined hands between my legs. My heart thrashes as I wonder what he's about to do in this busy classroom.

He doesn't stick them up my skirt like I expect — or hope. Instead, he grabs the seat of my chair and slowly drags me toward him. The chair scratches on the floor and all eyes turn to us. I feel the heated stare of someone who I can only guess is Seraphina, but I don't bother looking. Raphael doesn't appear to notice the commotion he's just caused. His eyes are only for me.

He stops once I'm close enough, my knees pressing against the seat of his chair and his legs straddling mine.

With my hand firmly in his, he says, "Try again."

How am I supposed to concentrate when he's so close? The scent of sandalwood and citrus surrounds me, burrowing its way past my defenses until I think I'll recognize his heady aroma anywhere.

Taking a deep breath, I close my eyes and focus on Raphael. The gently calloused feel of his hand in mine, the warmth of his thighs as they press against me, and the light, bubbly feeling I get in my chest when he's this close to me. When I think I'm ready, I press out with my thoughts and pray he can hear them.

You know, you light up the room too.

I know the moment he hears me. His eyes darken to match the deep-blue ring around his irises, and for just a moment I think he'll pull me into his arms right there in the middle of class.

Instead, the teacher comes over to our desk and I realize we're the only students left in the room.

"Well done, you two. Your connection will prove beneficial to you both in this class. Keep up the good work."

I smile and pull away from Raphael. The connections I'm forming here are unlike anything I've experienced outside of Dina. On one hand, I'm making friends that don't seem to care about my differences, but there are still so many students who think I'm a plague to the school.

How am I to trust that my new friends won't switch sides? I can't, not really. But I also can't go into every friendship with such negative energy. If I'm constantly waiting for the other shoe to drop, it won't be long before it does.

I won't turn my nose up at the only people who've shown me kindness here. I'll be as authentically me as I can and just hope they'll stick around.

"Got any plans right now, sunshine?" Raphael asks, shaking me from my melancholy.

"Not exactly, no. Unless you count avoiding assholes as a plan."

He smiles. "Come on then. You're joining Theo and me for a picnic."

"I'd love to," I reply, trying my best not to show my surprise at the mention of Theo. The more I think about it, the more it makes sense now why Theo was so kind to me. Raphael must have told him about our meeting in the cafeteria. Whatever he saw that day must have been good enough not to scare them away, even with all the drama. Whatever the reason, I'm grateful for it.

There's something special about the friends I've made so far. Raphael with his charm and wit, and Theo with his kind thoughtfulness. Even Zeke holds a magnetism that draws me to him like the others, though I haven't seen him since I slipped from his room.

My day may have started with catastrophe, but a picnic with new friends is exactly what I need to turn it around.

9

RAPHAEL

She agreed!

I can't stop the smile that spreads across my face as I type out a quick text to Theo, letting him know my plans. So what if we'd already decided to let her get settled first before we invited her to hang out with us? After what happened today, that angel deserves a break.

Raphael: I might have done a thing...

Theo: A good thing or a bad thing?

Raphael: Well we're now having a picnic with Hayliel. Like right now. So I'd say it's a damn good thing. Can you pack up some food?

Theo: On it. Meet me at the Knowledge house kitchenette.

We exit the Tower, and I look at Hayliel with a mischievous grin. "Want to fly with me to Knowledge house?"

She looks around, hesitating, before giving me a determined nod. That's my girl. Well, alright, so she's not *mine* exactly, but damn do I want her to be.

Our wings break free of our backs and through the slits designed in our school uniforms. With both of our backpacks in one hand, I reach out with my other to Hayliel. When she takes my hand, we run. Our wings flap once, twice, and we're in the air, soaring high above school ground and the old wishing well.

When I look at Hayliel, the smile on her face could outshine the sun. Pure joy radiates from her, and I can't help the satisfaction that flows through me.

As we land at the far side of Knowledge house, I almost can't move. The sight of Hayliel's windswept hair and pink-cheeked face has me wanting to fall to my knees and worship her for the rest of my existence. Theo opens the side door and waves us in, stopping me from making a fool of myself.

Once we're inside, Theo grabs a few items from the pantry, which Hayliel immediately helps him unload onto the table.

"Theo, this is Hayliel. Hayliel, this is my best friend, Theo."

"We met, actually," Hayliel replies, shooting a small smile toward Theo that has my chest squeezing. "We have History together. He saved me from what would have been a rather painful experience with a desk."

"Anyone would have done the same," Theo tells her, then frowns when he sees her raised eyebrow. "Er, maybe not. But it was nothing."

I press my lips together, not wanting them to see how stunned I am by that news. My muscles tighten as the burning sensation in my chest turns hotter while I obsess over the time they spent together. But isn't that what I wanted? Theo is as antisocial as they come, so I should be happy that he's taken a liking to her. And after what she's been through today, I'm sure she could use all the allies she can get.

Shaking off my selfishness, I take a deep breath and focus on the fact that my best friend and the angel of my dreams are getting along. Right now, that's enough for me.

Hayliel steps farther into the kitchen while Theo adds more food to an already overflowing basket. My mouth waters as I think about all the yummy things I bet he has in there. This is exactly what I need, just a taste of something delicious to keep my charm levels up, but when I reach for it, Theo slaps my hand.

"Oh, no, you don't. I only just got everything to fit. There's no way I'm letting you dig around in there." He takes the basket off the table and carries it outside.

"Psst."

Hayliel stands in the middle of the kitchenette with her hand behind her back. She pulls it forward to reveal a juicy red apple, passing it to me then placing her finger over her lips as if it's our little secret. *Fuck, what this angel does to me!*

Theo enters the room again, grabbing the blanket off the back of the chair before turning to me. I bring the apple up to my lips and take a bite out of it. Juice drips down my chin, and I almost groan.

"Where did you—"

"Your house is beautiful, Theo," Hayliel interrupts with a playful tilt to her lips.

I take another bite of my apple, looking at Theo to find out if he'll take the bait or not.

There's no fooling him, but he gracefully ignores my eating and steps toward Hayliel. "Thank you. Is it much different from your house?"

"Vastly different. But our kitchen has this white marble countertop too, except our cabinets are darker. I can show you both sometime, if you'd like?"

"We'd love that! Alright, come on you two. If we don't get this picnic started soon, I won't be held responsible for my charmless demeanor."

"Oh, no," Hayliel says, fake worry clouding her features. "I didn't realize things were that dire. Quick!" She pulls the blanket from Theo's hand and races out the door. We follow her out, only to find her standing there in the middle of the yard. "Where are we going again?"

"We know the perfect place. Follow us!" Theo and I let our white wings out, stretching them wide behind us, and I can't help but enjoy the look of awe on Hayliel's face when she sees us.

It quickly falls as she looks around, likely worrying about who will see her wings and what they'll say.

"Fuck them," Theo says, drawing her attention back to us. "Fuck those assholes and anyone who makes you feel like you're not enough. Don't let them take who you are."

"He's right," I tell her. "If they have something else to say about it, they'll have to go through us. We've got your back, sunshine."

"Thank you." Tears well in her eyes, but she wipes them away before they can fall.

There's something about her that draws me in, capturing my attention and making me delirious. She wants to be loved for who she is, and that's something I can relate to. *Don't we all just want to be accepted?*

With one more look around the yard, she lets her wings out, and we take to the sky. I claim the lead while Hayliel follows and Theo hangs back a bit, probably scouring the grounds for trouble.

We head to Somersault Falls. The giant waterfall spills from the tall rock face into a pool below. From the sky, I can see students already splashing in the water while others lie on the grass, basking in the sun.

The area between the Fallen house and the falls is almost empty, so I tuck my wings in slightly and dive.

"Holy shit," Hayliel says when we land as she stares at the roaring waterfall. Our distance muffles the sound, making it more soothing and less of a roar, so it'll be easier for us to talk amongst ourselves.

"Someday you'll have to jump off the top of the falls with us," Theo tells her as he takes the blanket from her arms.

She turns to us, her eyes wide. "People do that?"

I chuckle. "Why else would it be called Somersault Falls?"

"Come on. We'll tell you all about it over some food."

"You can't be serious!" Hayliel says with a laugh.

I smile, remembering the story. "Dead serious. I think my parents still have a copy of that newspaper at home."

"And they haven't taught alchemy since," Theo chimes in, sounding like he wishes they would start.

Hayliel pops another chip into her mouth, leaning back on her elbows with a calm look on her face.

Just then, an angel drops to the ground beside our blanket. Her dark, short, and spiky hair is unusual, yet oddly familiar.

"Dina!"

"I've been looking everywhere for you, babe. Now I find you've had a picnic without me?" Dina says, stealing a chip from the bag beside Hayliel. "How rude!"

"Theo, Raphael, this is my best friend, Dina."

"Nice to meet you. I'm glad to see you're eating well." Dina directs the last bit to me, and it hits me. This is the angel I met with Hayliel in the cafeteria. Fuck. I'd completely forgotten about her. My ears burn, but I shake it off and smile.

She turns to her friend, her face shrouded in worry. "You okay, Hayles?"

"Surviving. It would have been a lot worse without these two. I just hope it blows over soon."

"It will, babe. Are we still on for this weekend?"

"I wouldn't miss it for the world."

"Same. Alright, I've got a professor I need to charm. I'll catch you later." Her gaze shifts between Theo and me, assessing us both. "Hurt her and die, fellas."

Before she flies away, she smirks and throws a thumbs up to Hayliel, who only smiles wide in return. It's only when she catches on that I've seen everything that her cheeks turn pink, and I smother my chuckle.

"How long have you and Dina been friends?" Theo asks, reminding me he hadn't come over to meet them that day in the cafeteria.

Hayliel stares at her fingers, seeming far away from here as she thinks. "It feels like forever, honestly. I can't really think of a time when I didn't know her, but I know there was. I was fourteen, I think, and wildly distrustful. But she never gave up on me, and once I accepted that she wouldn't, we were insepa-rable."

She smiles, then shifts her gaze up to meet mine, and my heart seems to stall. Sunlight pours over my shoulders directly onto her face, turning her eyes from blue to gold for only a second before she lifts her hand up to shield herself. Never has there been a more realistic nickname than for this girl, my sunshine.

Theo lets his wings free, opening them to block the sun from her eyes, but I almost wish he hadn't. Seeing her bathed in sunlight makes something stir deep in my chest. It's unmistakable to name, yet potent enough that I want to bottle the feeling and always keep it with me.

I close my eyes, memorizing the image, and then let my wings out too. With the sun blocked, she drops her hand and gives us both a smile.

Theo clears his throat, and I wonder if he sensed the same thing as I did. "I'm glad you have a friend like that."

"And now you have us too." I wink and toss a grape in the air, effortlessly catching it in my mouth.

She giggles, and I can't help the rush of satisfaction I feel at the sound. Something moves in the distance behind her, and I focus my attention on it. An angel lands near the Fallen house, his large, black wings flapping slowly as he glares in our direction. *What the?*

Hayliel turns to see what I'm looking at, her smile widening for a beat before it falls. Had his stare turned colder when she looked at him or was my mind playing tricks on me? My legs ache to move, to confront the grumpy-ass angel and demand answers, but one look at Hayliel has me second-guessing.

She's pale now, her easy-going smile gone completely, and there's something behind her eyes that I can't interpret. What happened between this girl and an Assassins' Guild intern? And why do I want to know so badly?

Instead of asking the questions I'm so desperate to know the answers to, I focus all my attention on putting the light back in her eyes. That asshole may have wronged her, but it will be me who makes her glow again. Not him.

An understanding passes between Theo and me as our gazes lock. Hayliel is our friend now, and it's our duty to make her happy.

"So, sunshine ... How good of a swimmer are you?"

10

EZEKIEL

"What do you see, Ezekiel?" my lieutenant, Azrael, asks.

I know he'll want as many details as possible, so I take my time examining the scene before me. The Assassins' Guild is our strongest protection against the creatures who seek to harm us. It's made up of elite Fallen warriors who protect all of angelkind.

Ever since I was little, I've wanted to be part of the Guild. Both of my parents are members — well my dad still is, but my mother died after being kidnapped on a mission when I was six. Even so, it's always been a dream of mine. I'd rather fight and die alongside my fellow Fallen warriors than serve a Pure.

We've received more frequent calls recently that require all hands on deck and, as one of their top ranking interns, it's often I have to rush out to a scene with my commanding officer. This time is no different.

We stand in a modest Pure home in the forest bordering the housing district. The door is busted and hanging haphazardly off its hinges. Picture frames lie scattered alongside torn pillows and toppled furniture.

At first glance, I might have written it off as a run-of-the-mill attack. Not that those are common, but the divide between Pure and Fallen has flourished over the last decade or so, and the lone Fallen feather near the door is as good an indicator as any.

But this attack wasn't normal. Two bodies lie strewn across the floor, the walls surrounding them painted with strange, rune-like symbols I've never seen before, let alone understand. I reach out, wiping the tip of one finger through the dark liquid and bring it to my nose, breathing deeply. As the acrid scent hits my nose, I recoil. That isn't paint. It's demon blood.

Something flashes in the corner of the room, and I approach it carefully. A beautiful sun blade glints in the late afternoon sun, and I fall still.

There aren't many of those blades left throughout Silver City, and we reserve the ones we have for high-ranking Guild members. So what is it doing here?

I say as much to my lieutenant, who only nods, his lips turned down in a frown. Black blood coats the tip of the blade, and when I pick it up, ashes drift off it. There's a reason sun blades are so important to the Guild. It's the only weapon we have against demons.

Whichever beings created them are long since gone from this world, and that means we have to make do. But if this was here, surrounded by ash ... It could only mean one thing.

"A demon was here, just like at the other attacks. This blade explains the black feather we found by the door. If that's the case, though, where's the Guild member, and why did they leave the blade behind?"

"Precisely what I want to know. This is the third attack in as many weeks. What makes this one special?"

I look around the room once more, wanting to make sure I haven't missed anything. The first attack only involved breaking and entering an empty warehouse in the production district, but demon blood was found on the doorframe. The second attack moved inward to the outskirts of the entertainment district, but it failed too, the Pure having escaped with his life. This couple wasn't so lucky. When I'm confident I've seen it all, I turn back to my superior. "The difference is death. There's a pattern here, sir. The attacks appear to be moving toward more populated areas. With the high Pure and student population in the surrounding districts, perhaps we should consider increasing their patrols while also planning for a possible evacuation?"

"I appreciate your feedback, Ezekiel, but the evidence is inconclusive at best. I can't pull men from their stations on a whim. We'll continue to study the attacks and follow protocol until we have more to go on."

I nod, though I'm not at all convinced he's right. But I know better than to keep pushing the subject.

We continue investigating the apartment but find little else that can help us. Guild records should show which member they dispatched here, and hopefully that will provide us with more information. For now, though, my work here is done.

"Great work today. You've got a knack for detail, and it would appear that's exactly what we need to make it through whatever plan the demons have for us. I'll be in touch."

As is customary for my internship, I'll need to write up a detailed report on our findings, but my mind won't stop churning. There's a darkness hovering over us, and I'm no longer confident that angels will make it out unscathed.

Weary and worn, I fly over SCU on the way back to my dorm room. The school year has only just begun and already I'm tired. Angels are on edge with the attacks, and the local news stations are only fueling the frenzy.

Some of their fears have merit, even I can admit that. Somehow the demons are making it past Guild defenses, and at this rate, we'll only continue to fail unless we get more members.

But who will join us? The Pure certainly won't risk their lives for everyone the way we have. Who else will protect the citizens of Silver City if not for us Fallen? I suppose they don't really give us a choice in the matter. Outside of the Guild, Fallen jobs are more grunt work than anything else, even with a degree from a prestigious school like SCU.

The sun sits low on the horizon, casting stunning rays of light across the academy grounds as evening approaches. My stomach rumbles loudly, reminding me I forgot to eat lunch today. *Fuck, I'm starving.*

The sight of the Fallen house brings a smile to my face as I think about the hot shower and good meal I'll have tonight, but a familiar head of brown hair catches my eye. *Perhaps I can eat something else instead.*

Hayliel sits on a large blanket laid out on the grass, the warmth of her smile evident even from up here. Images of her in my bed and screaming my name flash through my mind. For a second, I consider landing next to her, scooping her up in my arms, and bringing her back there. She slunk out of my room like a ghost this morning, not even giving me a proper goodbye.

I wish she'd told me about her wings. Maybe I could have protected her somehow. At the very least, I could have tried to give her as much time as possible before revealing them to the school.

Beside her sit two Pure angels, their wings spread wide to block the shafts of light, with a basket of food between them on the blanket.

My feet hit the ground much harder than I mean for them to as anger rises inside of me. Is this why she left me this morning, because she's already seeing someone? And not just any *someone*. A Pure. The thought causes old wounds to fester in my chest, the sting of betrayal fueling the fire in my veins.

One of her friends notices me staring, but I don't look away, even when Hayliel turns her head. Her eyes light up when she sees me, almost causing me to step back at the force of it, but I don't move. She used me, and now she's made her choice.

And it's not me.

My gaze turns harder, more frigid, as emotions war within me. She must be able to sense them, even from this great a distance, because the smile falls from her pretty lips. I turn away, heading toward the front door. I really should just fly up to my balcony, but I need to work off this anger. Even now, I want to go to her. To warn those fuckers to stay the hell away from her because she's mine. But even I know that idea is foolish. She isn't mine. We fucked once and now she's moved on.

Part of me hates myself for treating her this way. I don't want to be the dark cloud looming over her and stealing her happiness. She couldn't have known that I've been in this exact situation before not too long ago and still haven't gotten over it. So what did she expect from me? That I'd be grateful for the chance to be in her presence, even for a short time, and not care that she's flaunting her new relationship in my face so soon after we slept together?

Shit. I *was* grateful though, wasn't I? Fuck.

A stack of school newsletters, the *SCU Weekly Observer*, sits beside the door. Last year these came out once a week, beginning on the second Monday of the school year, so they must have typed up a special edition for today. From the front-page headline, it's clear why. *New Student Has First Ever Gray Wings.*

Reaching down, I pull one from the top bundle and head up to the eighth floor, taking the stairs two at a time. Once inside my room, I perch on the chair in the corner and read the article.

New Student Has First Ever Gray Wings.
By Harold the Herald

It's the first day of a new term here at Silver City University, and we've already got a scandal. A freshman scholarship student showed up late to class this morning before proceeding to shock her classmates and professor by revealing her abnormalities. One student, Kristiel Pirie, even said she flaunted it. "It was obviously an attention grab. Why else would she strut up to the teacher, interrupt him, and let her dirty-looking wings free? I, for one, won't be giving her any."

Rumors spread throughout campus detailing other oddities witnessed, and even a few bone-chilling sights. Megan Waters, another first-year student, recounted a disturbing scene for this article. "I saw her horns in the bathroom. One second they were there, and then POOF. She'd forced them back into her skull. When our eyes met in the mirror, I could have sworn she licked her lips with a tongue that was three times the size of ours. A demon tongue, I'm sure of it."

Finally, we spoke with SCU's most promising student, Seraphina Beckett, to find out what she thought of the surprising start of term. "I'm hesitant to even say this, Harold, but I question the school's judgment. Letting an unknown creature onto school grounds is dangerous for the other students, especially with so many dis-

tressing accounts from my fellow classmates. We need to protect the next generation of angels. If it were up to me, she would face immediate expulsion."

So who is she, you might ask? The name of the strange new student is Hayliel Gracelin. Stay tuned for more about this mysterious development in our next column.

This is horseshit.

I crumple up the paper in my fist, all the while stewing over its contents and my own reactions. Even though she proved herself to be more like my ex than I ever would have thought, and despite the fact that it fucking hurts to be thrown aside, it doesn't make what they're doing right.

The world already treats us Fallen as lesser creatures, so who knows what kind of treatment she'll get now that they know she's even more different.

Regardless of the news running rampant at school, she managed to find two angels to stand by her side. As the days pass, I'm sure she'll find even more supporters who will accept her for who she is. Who wouldn't, after all?

Only a piece of shit, that's who.

That thought burrows its way deep inside me before taking root.

If I'm not careful, I'll become the very thing I hate.

11

HAYLIEL

I reread the passage, hoping it'll make sense this time, but no luck.

The Fallen library is quiet — too quiet — making it easy to get lost in my own thoughts instead of focusing on the task at hand. It's Sunday afternoon, almost a full week since classes have started, and I still haven't managed to get much sleep. After that stupid article in the *SCU Weekly Observer*, students have gotten braver. Half of my professors try to keep the peace, but the others just don't care. Sometimes it feels like they even egg it on, paving the way to a cruel joke or taunt.

At night, battles dominate my dreams. Most of the time, I'm fighting demons, protecting those who taunted me even though

I'd rather watch them fend for themselves. But other times ... on the rough days like Tuesday, when it felt as though walking the halls was the equivalent of a Walk of Atonement to cleanse my sins, the dreams morph into nightmares. No longer do I fight the demons. Now I'm one of them, their leader, and the smile that spreads across my mutated face is wicked with triumph.

Fuck. It's no wonder I'm exhausted.

Thank the Archangels for my new friends though. Theo and Raphael have been my constant companions. They stand by my side as often as they can, acting as my shields against the cruel words aimed at my chest. Somehow, they even succeed at making me smile. Their acceptance knows no bounds, even offering to assist in my search to find out what the fuck makes me so different. Who would have thought Pures could be so, well, *pure.*

As always, Dina has my back too, though with her second-year class load, I know she's doing her best. We had a study session in her room yesterday — which, as luck would have it, is just across the hall from mine — locked away from the prying eyes of everyone else. I left her feeling hopeful, like things were getting back on track and returning to normal. But with me, things never really are.

I've only seen Zeke a few times since I crept from his room. The first time was near Somersault Falls while sitting with Raphael and Theo. The way he'd looked at me then, like I'd torn the heart straight from his chest and pummeled it to the ground ... I saw more than just his anger that day. Buried beneath it was a world of betrayal. But what had I done to betray him? Is it because I left in the middle of the night? Or that my wings aren't the standard black that everyone assumed? None of it makes sense.

His demeanor didn't change when I saw him again on Wednesday or even last night after grabbing a snack from the kitchenette.

I flip ahead a few chapters in my book, desperate to find something that might help explain why I'm different. *Maybe then I can get the assholes to leave me alone.*

I read the text, skimming the parts about Pure angels being named for their purity, and the Fallen for their lack thereof.

At birth, angels are judged by the ruling Archangels to determine their true character. If they deem you pious and honorable, you'll receive wings of untainted white. But if they decide you aren't, those same wings will rot, turning black to match your sinful nature.

I scoff and shut the book, annoyed with the constant assumption that Fallen angels are corrupt and immoral. What the hell would that even make me, then, if I followed this logic? Only a little sinful? It's unlikely I'll find anything worthwhile in this stack, considering the last three I read were new versions, written after the Archangels overthrew our old God.

I pick up the last book anyway, not wanting to leave a single stone unturned. The paper feels different in this one, more textured and grainy than the others. It could mean this volume is older, perhaps from a time when God ruled Silver City, or it could just be a cheaper quality book. Either way, I squash down any hope rising to the surface and start reading.

There's more of the same discussion of Pure and Fallen, our differences and similarities, though this text is written in a much more positive light. As I flip through the pages, there's mention of the different types of angels like the ones we talked about in class last week.

The hierarchy of angels is a tenuous thing, but the list below is one we've created through exhaustive research and analysis.

God

Seraphim

Archangels

Cherub

Pure and Fallen

If I needed any further evidence that Pure and Fallen angels are equals, this text is it. Why isn't this used in our regular teachings? I make a mental note to talk to Professor Castiel about it, then keep reading.

While all celestial beings are considered immortal, we unfortunately have a few vulnerabilities. The Pure and Fallen, for example, won't die from a wound made with a steel blade or other man-made weapon, but an angel blade will harm them beyond repair. If a Pure or Fallen loses their wings to one of those blades, they will not grow back. But an angel blade won't harm the Seraphim, Cherub, or

I turn the page, desperate to read more, only to find the next few pages have been torn out. One small piece of the page remains with only one word on it. *Smiting.* What the hell is smiting, and why were the pages explaining our vulnerabilities ripped out?

The desire to scream in frustration rises, but I curb it, not wanting to interrupt any other students in the library. Instead, I pack up my books and head to the shelves.

As I put the last one back, I see a familiar head of dark hair from the corner of my eye. Zeke stands from his table and heads off down a row of books on the opposite side from me.

A spurt of confidence comes out of nowhere, urging me to talk to him and find out once and for all what the fuck is going on between us. Instead of walking over like a normal person, I creep on silent feet like a thief.

Books cover the table on an array of different subjects, from demon history to angelic rituals and weapons. In one book, there's a roughly drawn sketch of a sword, with the words *sun blade* below it. *Is this what they teach us in second year?*

Just as I'm about to step back and stop snooping, his slate pings with an alert from the Assassins' Guild, letting Zeke know there's been another attack and he's due to meet his superior within the hour.

Fuck. Another one. Throughout my entire existence, we've never experienced this many attacks in such a short period of time. I haven't quite figured out why yet, but each time we receive a news report about it, Theo's demeanor shifts. I've considered just asking him, but figure he'll open up to me when he's ready.

"What are you doing?"

At the sound of his deep voice, every atom in my body turns to molten lava.

"I just wanted to talk, but you walked away when I arrived." When I finally gather the courage to look up, I find the same icy expression from the day of the picnic. I flinch away, wounded by his glare.

"There's nothing to talk about. I have to get back to this." He places a new book on the table and sits in his chair like I don't even exist. *Ouch.*

I watch as he flips through the book, tracing the words with his long, masculine fingers before scribbling something on his slate. Stepping back, I force myself to retreat before I blurt out an offer to help with his research. He doesn't want me here. He said so himself.

That knowledge hurts more than I care to admit. I've been a fool, dreaming of the normal life I'd have here where no one knew my secret. As if students wouldn't find out and treat me as they always did. Like shit. And what does it say about me that I fell into bed with the first angel who showed me any attention?

Wandering back to the shelves, I pick out another few books and head to my table. It's exactly how I left it, with a bottle of water and my slate sitting in the middle. I should really be more careful with my things. After everything else these bullies have done to me so far, stealing my belongings isn't far from the list of possibilities.

Shaking it off, I open up the book on wing history and let thoughts of Zeke and the school assholes fall from my mind. I read and read, searching feverishly for anything that might help, but come up blank.

It's clear they wrote this book after the fall of God. Most of it is just compliments written about the Archangels and how much better they are than us lowly *normal* angels because they have an extra set of wings. *Big fucking whoop.*

Defeated, I cradle my head in my arms as doubt spirals in my mind. There's nothing for me to find here. I might have found some useful information in that book from earlier if someone hadn't ripped out the pages.

I hear Mom and Dad in my mind, their reassuring optimism stinging slightly. *Don't give up now, Haylie-bear. You're still finding little bits of information, and even the smallest detail can lead to great discoveries.*

I focus on my breathing, just like they taught me, breathing deeply in and out to settle myself. The negative thoughts lift from my mind and I can breathe a little easier, but I don't lift my head. With my eyes closed, I stay suspended in time, and before I know it, I drift off to sleep.

I startle awake to an empty library. Damn, I really am tired, aren't I? *At least the nightmares stayed away this time.*

Wiping my mouth, I'm grateful not to find any drool, but I'm sure there's a rather prominent arm imprint on my forehead.

As I shift, I feel a weight on my back that hadn't been there earlier. *What the hell?*

I reach behind me and find a jacket draped across my shoulders. When I pull it toward me, I'm enveloped in the familiar scent of leather with just a hint of something floral that I can't place.

The only person who'd been in the library before was Zeke. But why would he have done it? Based on our interaction earlier and the fact he's been ignoring me this past week, it's more than likely that he wouldn't notice me at all.

Deciding not to bother worrying about it, I check my slate to find a missed text from Raphael.

Raphael: Up for another picnic tonight, sunshine? Theo can't make it, so you're stuck with just me.

I smile, my mood shifting entirely from this one message.

Hayliel: Who could turn down food? It's a date *drool emoji*

The moment I hit send, my stomach drops. Fuck. Why did I have to put the drool emoji after the date part? It clearly should have gone after the food part. I probably shouldn't have even said the date bit at all.

While I put away the books and pack up my things, I try not to let my worries get the best of me. After all, it's possible he didn't notice. Right?

12

EZEKIEL

These new markings worry me. From what Dad says, runes and rituals aren't really a demon thing, or at least they haven't been in the past three hundred years.

The library is quiet, and images of Hayliel sprawled out on the grass with her Pure boyfriends keep popping into my brain. I shake them off and throw myself into researching the runes.

I'm here to join the Assassins' Guild and avenge my mom. Nothing else matters. As much as I may need the distraction, this particular task is more like pulling out teeth. The Archangels had most of the books rewritten, and the few pieces of original text I found were scribbled out or ripped up.

With my frustration mounting, I stand and head back to comb through the texts once more. If I'm honest, this feels like a waste of fucking time. I stroll through the aisles, scanning each title for anything that might seem useful. Most of them are shit, but I find one that sounds promising and head back to read through it.

Before I step out from between two bookshelves, I find Hayliel looking at the texts I left laid out on the table. I watch as her eyes trace the details of the sun blade with curiosity. She tucks a strand of hair behind her ear, looking rather adorable in a purple Silver City University sweater. Part of me wishes I could talk to her, tell her everything I know and see what she thinks, but I'm still angry.

At her. At myself. At those pieces of shit from the school newsletter. And even at those Pure boys for offering the support to her that I can't seem to manage. I know it's misplaced, but it's there all the same.

The low lighting in the library brings out the dark circles beneath her eyes. As angels, we can handle a ton of shit that mortals can't, and it takes a lot to wear us out. So what the hell is keeping her up at night? I shake off my worry, though, because she's strong. I knew it from the moment we first met, and every encounter with her so far has only solidified it. For all I know, her little Pure groupies are the reason that she's so tired. If she screams for them as much as she did for me …

My slate pings with a notification, interrupting my train of thought. I watch as Hayliel reads the pop up, her brow furrowing from whatever she sees.

"What are you doing?" I ask, causing her to freeze. Keeping my face blank, I walk back to my spot and do my best to ignore her.

"I just… wanted to talk, but you walked away when I arrived." She finally looks up at me, stepping back as our eyes lock. Maybe I haven't done such a good job at keeping my face neutral after all.

"There's nothing to talk about. I have to get back to this." It takes every ounce of willpower I have not to push the books off this table and fuck her until this all blows over.

She wants to talk? Like we can be friends after she brushed me aside for something better? All I want to do is fuck some sense into her and show her just what she's missing out on. But I don't. Instead, I sit back in my chair and crack open my book like it's the most interesting thing in the fucking world. Like her sweet, earthy scent isn't making me lose my goddamn mind.

I jot something down in my slate, pretending to find the information in this dusty old tomb wholly fascinating when in reality, I can't keep my thoughts off the luscious angel beside me. Fuck. If she doesn't leave soon, I might do something we'll both regret.

As if she can hear my thoughts, she walks away. The air around me feels colder with her gone, like she's taken all the warmth with her. The longer she's gone, the less the air tastes of honeyed sugar. But as I try to focus on my research again, one thought keeps niggling at the corners of my mind. *What if this is all a big misunderstanding and she actually wants me?*

The light on my slate flashes, reminding me of the notification from earlier. A message from the Guild. Shit. Another attack, and I'm needed in an hour.

I've still got a few minutes before I have to leave though, so I push aside all thoughts of one very special gray-winged angel and focus.

The book in front of me is another rewritten text, but this one details an old historic account of the first demons in Silver City. Instead of God removing them from our land, it states the Archangels were responsible.

No one truly knows how demons came to be. Our old textbooks might have told us they've always existed, even saying they co-existed with us, but we know that to be false; a lie woven into old stories to fool us. It is our understanding that demons only came to be from our corruption. Since the dawn of time, angels have been tempted by the sinful and the wicked. Each of us fought that desire and chose purity over all else until one day, they didn't.

I keep reading, falling deeper into the realization that this book is basically just 'he said, she said.' Whether the old God was right or the Archangels are, I have no clue, but I don't have the fucking time to figure it out.

This volume was the last hope I had of finding something without visiting the Knowledge house. Their library is at least three times the size of ours. It's foolish of me, but I hate needing the Pures for anything.

With a sigh, I gather up the books and put them back on the shelves, trying my best not to think about Hayliel and the fact that she might still be here.

It's Sunday afternoon. I'm sure she has better things to do than sit in here alone.

Slipping my slate into the inner pocket of my leather jacket, I head toward the exit but stop when I hear a soft whimper from the back corner. I should ignore it and leave, but my legs keep moving forward until I see her. Hayliel.

Slumped over on the desk, she rests her head on her arms, her hair fanned out around her. What the hell is she doing in here? She should sleep in her room, not in this cold, drafty library. I consider waking her and telling her just that, but she seemed so worn out earlier.

Her relaxed face shifts into something like discomfort as she releases another soft whine. My heart nearly shatters at the sound, and I'm helpless to the need pulling me forward. My finger dances gently across her forehead until she relaxes once more.

I can't just leave her here like this.

Pulling my slate from the pocket of my jacket, I check the time to make sure I won't be late for the Guild before placing it quietly on the table beside her. She doesn't move as I take off my jacket and drape it across her back.

The sight of her in my clothes turns my dick rock solid. I wish I could see the look on her face when she wakes up. Will she know it was me? Will she wear my jacket around campus? I hope she does. I fucking hope she wears it in front of her Pure boyfriends too.

Maybe then they'll know they aren't the only ones with a claim on her.

13

HAYLIEL

The gentle breeze of a warm evening caresses my feathers as I fly. Tucking in my wings, I swoop down toward the dock where Raphael waits. When I land, I can't help the sharp intake of breath as I survey the setup in front of me.

Past the dock, draped across the sand, lies the same thick blanket from our last picnic. Raphael sits in one corner with a basket of food on the opposite one. Beyond him, the sky is bright with red, pink, and orange as the sun slowly sinks down, appearing to slip beneath the waves. I'm glad I stopped by my room to change before coming out. There's no need for sweaters or some stranger's leather jacket here.

"Holy shit. You did all of this?"

"*This* was all me," he says, gesturing to the picnic. "But I had no part in the beautiful views here tonight."

He stares at me as he speaks, like he hasn't noticed the gorgeous setting sun behind him and instead, he's referring to me.

Something pricks in my chest, but not in a bad way. I feel alive in his presence, and not just because my heart thuds within my ribcage and the blood pumps quickly through my veins. It's more than that, and it's something I want to hold on to for as long as I'm able.

"Have you started eating without me?" I tease, taking the spot beside him that faces the ocean. He looks comfortable here on the beach with his platinum-blond hair, blue eyes, and a smattering of freckles across the bridge of his nose. I bet he has more in the summer, too.

"I couldn't very well show up here and embarrass myself again. What would you think of me then?" He says the words with a smile, like he's trying to play it off as a joke, but I see beyond the clever mask.

Reaching forward, I clasp his hand in mine, squeezing gently. "I don't like you because of your charm and fancy words. You're so much more than that. Plus, your embarrassment is kind of cute."

"So what you're saying is you like me and think I'm cute." He squeezes my hand back, looking completely satisfied with the direction of our conversation.

I laugh, rolling my eyes at him because, of course, that's what he'd focus on. Even though I don't want to, I pull my hand back from his and rub them together. "I'm starving. What did you bring me?"

His blue eyes sparkle as he sifts through the basket before pulling out two ham and swiss croissants, a bottle of sparkling apple cider with two paper cups, and a plate of chocolate dipped strawberries.

My jaw damn near drops to the blanket. "Correct me if I'm wrong, but none of this is on the school menu. Where the hell did you get this from?"

He smirks, running a hand through his hair like he's satisfied with himself. "I might have convinced the lunch lady to let me plunder her pantry and spent all afternoon in the kitchen trying to make everything perfect."

Heat emanates from my chest, spreading through my limbs with a speed I can't control. He did all of that for me? "I ... Raphael. That's the nicest thing anyone's ever done for me. Thank you."

His ears turn pink, but the wide smile stays trapped on his face, showing off his pearly-white teeth. "Maybe don't thank me until you've eaten some of it. If it's bad, we can just blame Esme."

"Deal. But I'm sure it'll be delicious." I reach for a strawberry, grabbing hold of the leafy green end before taking a bite. Fuck, these are good. I moan, savoring the sweet taste while seriously considering grabbing another.

Raphael only watches, his eyes a darker shade of blue now.

"Are you not having one?" I ask, almost breathless, though I can't figure out why. *Fine, that's a lie. I know damn well why, and it has everything to do with the angel in front of me.*

"We'll see. Have as many as you want. Would you like some cider?"

I nod and thank him before unwrapping the croissant, surprised to find it warm beneath my fingers. As I take a bite, flavors burst on my tongue, and I can't help but release another groan of satisfaction. I swallow, covering my mouth and say, "Raphael, this is fucking incredible."

He hands me a cup, tapping his own to mine. "To new friends."

"And talented cooks," I add, before taking a sip of the cool liquid. It's sweet and tangy, a perfect addition to the sandwich, and it's not long before I've devoured both.

Raphael finishes his too, but at a slower pace, and I think I should feel self-conscious. Girls aren't supposed to eat like heathens, are we? Either way, I can't find it in me to care.

There are only the strawberries left, and Raphael hasn't had a single one yet. I take a deep breath, mustering up the courage for what I have planned.

"You really should try one," I tell him, picking up a strawberry before getting to my knees and shuffling closer.

His eyes widen as I bring the fruit to his lips, and he doesn't hesitate before taking a bite. Damn, he has pretty lips. The bottom one is slightly fuller than the top, both of them slick with juice.

"See," I whisper, my body tingling at our nearness. How easy would it be to kiss him right now? To show him just how grateful I am for his friendship and everything he's done for me. But something holds me back. What if I've read the signs wrong? I don't think I can survive without his friendship.

I pull away slowly, forcing myself back to my spot on the blanket, and let him make the next move. Nothing has happened yet that we can't shake off. If he's not interested in me, then at least I won't make a fool of myself.

Raphael stays quiet, watching me as I grab another strawberry from the plate. I feel naked beneath his gaze. Exposed. To distract myself, I take a bite of the juicy berry, silently telling myself this is the last one. Just as I finish chewing, Raphael comes closer.

Slowly, he lifts his hand and wipes the corner of my lips with his thumb. I sit frozen in shock, barely breathing in case I might spook him. He's close, so close that the heat of his body glides across my skin, and I don't want him to move away again.

He brings his thumb to his mouth, sucking off the chocolate he stole from my lips. "Delicious."

Fuck, that's hot. My heart thrums to an irregular beat, making me disoriented. It mixes with the need and desire until it feels like I've taken a shot of adrenaline.

He must feel it too because he grabs my face in his hands and kisses me, stealing the very breath from my lungs. My core clenches as he wraps his expert tongue around mine, shifting us both until I'm lying back on the blanket, not even caring that my head rests on the warm sand.

He pulls back a little, his eyes roaming over my face and down to my SCU T-shirt. "I've wanted to do that since the cafeteria."

Without replying, I kiss him again, pulling him into me and lifting my head to deepen it. I turn on my side, half considering straddling him right here and now, but I hold back. The judgy bitch in my head tells me I've done this already with Zeke and reminds me of how poorly that turned out. But Raphael isn't Zeke. He's been there for me when I needed him and I trust in that more.

As if he can read my mind, his kisses move south, down my neck and over my shirt, until his knees settle between my legs. He doesn't speak, but I read the question in his eyes well enough and nod, letting him know I'm okay with where this is going. By the wicked glint in his eyes, I know he'll have me begging in no time.

He pulls my shirt up, exposing me to him. My nipples pebble beneath his watchful gaze, but he doesn't move to touch me. Instead, he reaches for the sparkling juice, and I can't help but laugh.

"Thirsty, are we?" I tease. Things are always so light and carefree with Raphael. He makes me smile and laugh more than anyone ever has, and I've come to realize just how much that aspect has been missing in my life.

"Absolutely parched," he replies, unscrewing the cap.

Instead of taking a swig from the bottle like I expect, he pours the cool liquid carefully onto my bare skin. I yelp when it hits me, but don't move. There isn't a lot on me, just enough to pool between my breasts and trickle down the sides of my stomach.

My breath comes out in short pants, waiting to see what he'll do next. He doesn't make me wonder for long, dropping his head to lap up the liquid from my flesh. He licks me everywhere, regardless of where the juice is or isn't. The only place he doesn't touch is my nipples. I mewl, desperately needing more.

When he sits up and grabs the bottle again, I break.

"Raphael."

He takes a swig straight from the bottle of juice, then descends onto my nipple, wrapping his lips around the pointed bud and making me cry out. The contrast between his warm lips and the cold cider makes me giddy and desperate.

In a move so out of character that I shock even myself, I unbutton my jeans.

"Are you sure?" he asks me, and I want to scream and beg for him to take me, fuck me. Make me feel.

Instead, I nod. "I need you, Raphael." My voice comes out hoarse, as if I haven't spoken for days.

He moves to lie beside me, his muscular frame the only thing I can see. I grab hold of his shirt, pulling him down for a kiss and wishing he was far less clothed. I want to see his chest, learn the contours of his body until I know them as well as my own.

All thoughts stop when his hand teases at the waistband of my jeans, slipping beneath my soaked panties. He groans into my mouth, but I swallow the sound down with my own inhale.

Wasting no time, he coats his fingers in my arousal and presses one inside me, then another. I grip tighter to his hair as he moves, wanting to switch positions so I can touch him too.

He pumps faster, adding a third finger until the wet sounds of my pussy blend in with the waves crashing on shore. I'm soaring, my body nearing the precipice of ecstasy.

Reality crashes in around me as footsteps approach, followed by the sound of laughter.

My eyes fly open. People are coming this way. Shit. Shit. Shit!

Raphael's fingers don't stop. He drops his head, whispering in my ear. "I don't care who sees, sunshine. I'm not stopping until you come all over my fingers."

His words are fuel to my already raging fire, igniting my world until all I see are the flames.

I do my best to stay quiet, not wanting anyone to find us here. There's a small part of me that relishes in the possibility of getting caught, stirring deep in my core and enhancing my pleasure.

Raphael extracts a finger, leaving two inside of me, which he pumps feverishly, hitting a spot so deep that I can almost see stars. His thumb moves to my clit, gliding over my sensitive nub until it feels like I might explode.

Someone laughs again, closer this time, sounding almost directly on top of us, but still Raphael doesn't stop. And it's then that I reach the brink of my climax, swept away by the endless waves of it. My carefree angel kisses me, muffling the sound of his name on my lips.

After a moment, he pulls away and presses a kiss to the tip of my nose. "Would you believe that I'm hungry again?"

I can't hold back the laugh that erupts from my throat. Would it even be Raphael if he wasn't eating? But from the glint in his eyes, I realize he isn't talking about food.

He extracts his fingers from my jeans, leaving me to button them up right before a group of three students walks out on the dock. They don't look like the worst of my bullies — thank the Archangels for small victories — but I can't stop the blush from rising.

"Damn. A picnic is a great idea!" the shortest guy says, eying our setup.

Raphael only smiles, sucking on his fingers as if to rub it in their faces that they don't have a picnic. Except ... those fingers were inside me only moments ago.

"It really is," Raphael finally replies, his gaze trained on me instead of the newcomers, and I watch him clean off another digit with fascination. He's not wasting a single drop. "Best fucking thing I've ever tasted."

My pussy pulses, ready to go again, but this time I want to be the one making him lose control. And that's exactly what I'll do.

14

HAYLIEL

The locker room is quiet as I change into my combat gear. I arrived at the weaponry training building early, hoping to avoid getting stuck in here with someone like Seraphina and her minions.

Luck, it appears, is on my side. At least for now.

Despite this class being mandatory for all Silver City University students, I'd have chosen it as an elective anyway. Being able to protect myself is a skill I wish I'd known years ago.

I pull on the leggings before throwing on the matching long-sleeve spandex shirt, surprised to find the outfit covers so much. Not that I'm complaining. I have no idea what to expect from today, so I'll take all the barriers I can get.

Dina assured me over breakfast this morning that I'd be fine, but I receive enough hate around campus already. What the fuck will happen in a course specifically meant for fighting? Visions of me as the class punching bag fill my mind. Students throwing me around and abusing me under the guise of training. It's exactly what I'm expecting.

Anxiety grips me hard, so I focus on controlling my breathing and think about the picnic last night. Of Raphael's touch and the way he made me feel. It had been a perfect evening. Part of me was worried that things would be weird after, but he and Theo joined us for breakfast, and everything seemed perfect. Theo can be hard to read, but if he knew what Raphael and I had done last night, he didn't show it.

I exit the locker room and step into a long, narrow room filled with punching bags, mats, and other gear I've never seen before. The only other angel in here is the teacher, whose red hair and muscular frame remind me of a highland warrior I read about in a book from Earth. I make my way toward him and find a seat on the mats near the front.

"You're here early."

"I am. Being late hasn't served me anything but suffering." I don't mean for him to hear the last part, but things don't often go my way.

"Ah, right. You must be Hayliel then. I'm Professor Malik."

I blush, surprised that he knows who I am from just one sentence. I guess rumors really do spread fast in a school like this. "Nice to meet you."

"To survive in my class, Miss Hayliel, all you need to do is show up on time and do your best. I have a no-bullshit policy here, and if anyone breaks that rule, they'll be put in their place. Do you understand?"

I nod in agreement, even though I don't really. I can't tell if he's warning me about causing bullshit or offering me support in a backward sort of way.

The classroom fills up quickly, and I'm happy not to find any of my usual tormentors among the faces here. Professor Malik waits another moment before introducing himself, but before he can give out instructions, the door to the changing room opens and a familiar face walks in.

Zeke.

What the hell is he doing here?

"Class, this is Ezekiel Oren, a student at SCU and one of the Assassins' Guild's interns. He'll be joining our classes on a regular basis to assist with your training. Within these walls, he's to be treated the same as any faculty member. Do I make myself clear?"

"Yes, Professor," the class chimes in unison.

"Good. We'll begin with basic maneuvers. Ezekiel and I will demonstrate, and then you'll spend a bit of time practicing yourself. After that, we'll partner you up for some one-on-one training. As this is your first year, we'll be taking things slow, assessing to find out where your strengths lie and where you need the most focus. Now. Let's begin."

Professor Malik and Zeke each stand in front of a punching bag, calling out different hits and kicks before performing the action. I can't tear my eyes away from the firm muscles of Zeke's body. Even beneath the tight fabric of his combat gear, I can almost see each individual muscle and remember the way his body felt pressed into mine.

He looks up then, catching my ogling, and I have no doubt that he caught the lust behind my eyes. I could probably scorch his damn shirt off if I don't look away. *Get it together, Hayliel. Raphael quenched your damn thirst yesterday. Don't be greedy.*

When the professor shouts that it's time to try it ourselves, I push all thoughts of Zeke aside and practice the strikes as they're called out.

"Jab!"

This one is easy enough. I punch with my fist closest to the bag. A small grin spreads across my face, but I shake it off and focus on practicing the hit a few more times.

"Straight punch!"

Even easier. Using the hand furthest away from the bag, I twist my body to give me optimal power, feeling the swing of my ponytail with the motion. *Piece of fucking cake.*

The small hairs on the back of my neck stand up, and something tells me I'm being watched, but as I survey the room, everyone's concentrating on their strikes. Professor Malik and Zeke make their way through the class, throwing out tips on stance as they go.

"Hook punch!"

I don't have a lot of experience with fighting, but Dina had taken a boxing class when she was younger before the instructor moved away and the new one wouldn't take Fallen students. She and I would practice whatever she'd learned in class that day, and this one had always been my favorite.

Once I've thrown the punch a few times, that odd sense of being watched comes back. I can feel the heat of the stare along my cheek. Pretending to throw another punch, I turn, my gaze locking on Zeke's green eyes across the classroom.

He clearly wants nothing to do with me, so why the fuck does he keep staring? I ignore him, focusing on the commands the professor calls out as we move from punching to kicking. It feels good to get some of this energy out, and by the time we've finished our rounds on the bag, I feel lighter than I have in a long time. As hard as I try, though, I can't quite shake the watchful gaze of Zeke. Especially not when he continues to stray closer to me.

"Great job, class. Before you split into pairs and pick a mat, Zeke and I will show you a few practical takedowns, holds, and basic sparring techniques we'd like you to familiarize yourself with."

Once again, I'm forced to watch Zeke's powerful frame. They take turns throwing or holding one another, and I can't help the drool that pools in my mouth while watching Zeke throw down. If only he'd take his head out of his ass, then maybe I'd let him toss me around like that. Okay, maybe that's not exactly true. My pussy would for sure, but with whatever's going on between Raphael and me, I doubt he'd appreciate me fucking someone else.

How the hell have I ended up in this situation?

The pair finish up their demonstrations, and Professor Malik addresses the class. "Once you've got a partner and a mat, you may get started. We'll work on this for the rest of the class. Begin!"

The students break up into groups around me, each pair running off to claim their mat and preparing to test out their new tactics, but not a single person approaches me. No one even looks my way until it's clear I'm the only one without a partner.

It stings, and I'm reminded that as great as things have been going with my friends, everything outside of our little group is still shit.

"Ah, I thought I saw we'd have an odd number of students," Professor Malik says when he approaches me. "Zeke, could you come here, please?"

Zeke finishes helping a pair of doe-eyed girls with their form before heading our way, and the blood in my veins starts to boil. Why does seeing him with other girls affect me so much? It's not as though I have any claim to him, and he's made it perfectly clear that he wants nothing to do with me. But why can't I shake him and this unmistakable jealousy?

Zeke finally approaches us, his brows drawn together when he realizes Professor Malik stands beside me.

"I need you to pair with Hayliel."

Zeke's face never shifts, seeming completely neutral except for the small crease between his brows. We speak at the same time.

"I have to assist the other students."

"Oh no, that's really not necessary, Professor. I can just keep practicing with the bag or find someone outside of class to help me with the holds." *Throwing myself repeatedly to the ground might even work, if it gets me out of working with the guy who hates me.*

Zeke's expression changes then, but I struggle to read the look on his face. The way he glares at me now makes me think he's angry, but why? We're both doing the same thing here. Trying to convince the professor to let us do our own thing instead of forcing us into a situation clearly neither of us wants.

"You will both work together on this if you want to receive a credit in my class. Do I make myself clear?"

"Yes, Professor," we say in unison.

"Good. This is a great opportunity for you both. Don't waste it." Then Professor Malik strolls away.

An awkward silence falls over us that I try to shake off.

"Do you have a preference?"

I glance up at him, my eyes wide. "I'm sure we'd both rather work with other people, but you heard the professor. We don't have a choice."

The corner of his lip turns up slightly before he says, "With the mats. Do you have a preference with the mats?"

"Oh ..." *Well, that's not embarrassing.* "Is there one far enough away from the other students so I won't find an *accidental* foot on my back?"

His brows crease once more, something like concern flashing behind his eyes for a second before it's gone. "That would never happen."

"You'd be surprised," is all I say in response as I spot the perfect mat. I don't bother waiting for Zeke as I make my way toward it. He likely wouldn't believe me, anyway. His odd treatment of me started on the first day of classes, the same day I showcased my wings. It doesn't take a genius to figure out why he's pissed at me. He's mad that he fucked the weird demon student.

I stand on the mat, stretching out my arms and legs while I wait for Zeke to join me. When he does, he watches me intently but says nothing.

"What do we do first, Professor Zeke?"

He smiles at the title, and I can't stop the matching one that grows on my face. If I'm supposed to treat him as any other professor, then that means he's off limits. But does that really matter when I've already had one delicious taste of him?

"I want you, Miss Hayliel, to take me to the ground."

He talks slowly, accentuating every word. My mind gets stuck on the first three, and I'm unable to get the image of me straddling him on this very mat out of my head.

I rush forward, trying to tackle him straight out, but he only shifts aside and pushes me to the ground. I land on my stomach with Zeke's body pressed up against my back.

"I'm not going to let you win that easily, hummingbird," he whispers into my ear before withdrawing, taking the heat at my back with him.

My heart pumps wildly at the sound of his nickname for me. His words only spur me on, making me more desperate to bring him to his knees.

I jump to my feet, turning to watch him. We walk in circles, neither of us wanting to take our eyes off the other for even a second.

Darting toward him, I feint left, then go right as I try to trip him, but it's like he can see me coming. Once again, I land on the mat, but this time he doesn't fall with me.

"You should really hide your tells better."

"Aren't you supposed to be helping me?" I mutter as I stand, feeling useless.

Instead of showing me like I'd hoped, he only says, "You watched Malik and I. What do you think you're doing wrong?"

Closing my eyes, I think back on their demonstration and realize I've been trying to tackle him to the ground like we're playing the human version of football, but that isn't what they want.

Before my eyes are even open, I use my back leg to propel me forward. I grab his shirt, step past him to send him off-balance and then kick my left leg into his so he topples to the floor.

"Yes!" I shout, doing a little dance while Zeke lies sprawled out on the mat, wearing a matching smile.

He grabs my leg, pulling hard until I'm falling across his chest. I land with an oomph, but Zeke seems completely fine.

"Save the victory dances until after you've secured your foe." He slaps my thigh, dangerously close to my ass, and I suck in a breath. "Again."

We spend the rest of the class practicing different hold techniques and takedowns, our bodies constantly pressed together in varying positions that only drive me mad.

It doesn't help that Zeke is acting more like himself — at least the one I knew before classes started. The playfulness is back, and I can't help but feel like maybe things will turn around. Maybe we can finally get to a place of friendship. My core flutters as he holds me to the mat once more, our faces mere inches apart and the thickness of his erection pressing deliciously against me. Alright, so my vagina clearly wants more than friendship.

"Zeke," I whisper, unable to keep the yearning from my voice. I'm surrounded by him. The scent of jasmine and leather fills my nose and clouds my mind with images of another night when we were this close.

He doesn't move, keeping me trapped beneath him, our breath mingling as we stare into each other's eyes. I wish I could read his mind, learn the thoughts hiding behind his green eyes. Is he thinking of our night together? The way our painted bodies fit so perfectly, just like they are now.

Class is done, yet still we don't move. I can't stand it, being in limbo with no idea of what we are to each other, or what he even wants.

"What is this between us?"

Whatever spell held us captive dissolves at my words. I watch as his eyes shift, morphing into something cruel and unrecognizable.

He stands abruptly, like he'd strayed too close to a fire and felt the scorching heat of the flames against his skin.

"Nothing. You made sure of that."

His words cut me open, just like I'm sure he intended they would. But more than that, they confuse me. What the fuck had I done to make him so angry?

"What the hell is your problem?"

He ignores my question entirely, and just when I think he'll leave without another word, he turns back. "Run along, little Hayliel. I'm sure the perfect little Pure boys you have wrapped around your finger are waiting to take you on another picnic."

He can't be fucking serious. He's pissed at me because I've made friends outside of the Fallen? As if I even have enough friends to be fucking choosy. My pulse beats wildly, the rush of blood drowning out everything else.

"You can pretend you're different, Zeke, but you're just like the fucking Pures. They treat us like shit, and it's exactly what you're doing. To them and to me. If you want to hate on everyone who doesn't look the same as you, that's not my problem.

And I'll take their fucking friendship over the conditions of yours any damn day."

I stalk past him, my anger propelling me forward until it feels like I might explode. Who the fuck is he to judge me, anyway? Without Theo, Raphael, and Dina, I'd be alone. An outcast. I won't let him make me feel like shit for letting someone else care for me, regardless of which social class they fall into.

But as I change out of my combat gear, a little voice inside my head whimpers.

I wanted him to care for me too.

15

THEO

The cool night air threatens shivers down my spine, but the warmth of the blazing bonfire chases it away.

To the left of us, the arena sits empty and dark. To our right, the weaponry training building has one lone light shining from what I can only assume is Professor Malik's office. Sitting next to the fire with Hayliel and Raph, I can almost believe we're the only three on campus.

We'd originally come here to burn as many of those fucking SCU newsletters as we could. Harold the Herald was at it again, this time speaking with other students who all said terrible things about the angel I now call a friend. We'd considered paying him a little visit, but Hayliel stopped us. "They just want a reaction. Drama. I'm inclined not to give it to them," she'd said. I can't argue with that.

Despite there being several empty benches around the fire, the three of us sit huddled on the same one. Raphael and I perch on either end with Hayliel in the middle, each of us roasting a marshmallow now that the burned newsletters have floated away on the breeze. Something about the moment just feels so *right*. Her sage-and-honey scent fills my senses, mixing with the smoke and sweets until I'm breathing in one addicting combination.

None of us care that the other students avoid us. Hell, I say it's a gift from the Archangels. More s'mores for us.

I don't really like other people, anyway. They're too talkative and nosey, like they deserve every ounce of my past just for existing. I never had an issue with Hayliel, though. I wonder why.

She laughs at something Raphael says, playfully swatting his arm while trying to keep her marshmallow from falling into the flames, and I can't look away. Her brown hair appears red against the glow of the fire, and when she smiles, it's like watching a meteor shower. Rare and beautiful.

If it were up to Raphael, he'd don a jester costume and be her own personal joker if it meant we'd see her happiness more. I'm starting to see his point.

"Oh, no! Rest in peace, Marshmallow King."

I shake my head, realizing now that Hayliel's grin is gone, replaced with a pout. She's looking at me like maybe I should be sad too, but I don't …

Then I see it. The flaming ball of goo at the end of my stick. I jerk it back and watch as the oozing fireball seems to hover in midair before falling to the embers with a plop.

"Here. You can have mine." Hayliel brings her own stick forward, revealing the perfectly toasted marshmallow. It's golden brown around the edges, creating a crunchy shell around the soft, gooey inside. But I can't eat her food. I let myself get distracted and burned my treat. It's no one's fault but my own.

"You don't have—"

She shoves the warm marshmallow into my mouth, interrupting my protest, and I can't help the moan that leaves me as flavors explode on my tongue. I watch as she sucks the leftovers off her fingers, and holy fucking shit. I feel drunk from her nearness.

"I made two for myself, but … I guess you can have one." Raphael holds out one of his marshmallows. His are more brown than golden, but she eats it from his hand anyway, her tongue darting out to lick one of Raphael's long, nimble fingers.

I swallow, wanting desperately to witness more of that before shoving the thought into a box so far at the back of my brain that I hope it'll never surface again.

"One of these days, you'll have to share your expertise with the class because that shit was incredible! For now, I guess I'm on cookie duty." I grab the box of chocolate-coated butter cookies and open the bag, focusing all my attention on prepping for the next s'more and not on the angel beside me.

A laugh leaves her while she places two more marshmallows onto her forked stick and hovers it over the fire. "Both of my parents are Fallen. They work in the factories, mostly with textiles. When I was growing up, we didn't have much money, but marshmallows were cheap so these were our go-to celebration snack. We'd normally eat them without the cookies, since those were an extra expense, but we perfected the toasting process. If we got sick of eating them toasted, we'd experiment until we found a fun, tasty new way to eat them."

I try to picture a younger version of Hayliel, sitting in front of a marshmallow with a candle protruding from it to celebrate her birthday. From everything she's told us about them, her parents seem like two of the most wholesome angels. The love they have for their daughter is unconditional, something I wish more parents could say. After what she's been through so far at school and likely before coming here, I'm glad she has them.

It's not long before the marshmallows are done and I use the cookies to take the toasted mallows off the stick, handing one to each of them. We eat our treats in comfortable silence, watching the fire pop and sparks fly.

Hayliel sticks her hand into the bag of marshmallows and hands one to each of us. Raphael immediately moves to impale it on his stick, but she stops him by laying her hand on his arm. "We're not going to toast these. We're going to tear them apart until they're all gooey."

She places a forefinger on the top of the mallow, her thumb on the bottom, and then her other hand follows the same position on the opposite side. Gently, she pulls and twists her fingers and the marshmallow until it turns from a solid shape into something far stickier. It's a mess.

Raphael and I follow her steps until white goop covers our fingers. Mine falls to the ground at my feet, and Raph makes such a fucking mess with his that he somehow smeared it all over his face. I clean the white ooze off my fingers, watching as Hayliel falls into a fit of laughter.

She jolts into me when Raphael lunges for her, his hands covered in white, gooey strands of half-melted marshmallow. I pick her up and dash around the bench as Raphael gives chase, but I don't try *that* hard, so it's no surprise when he catches up to us.

Instead of rubbing the sticky mess on her, he only leans forward and places a kiss on her lips before moving back to his seat on the bench. Her body shivers in my arms. Hell, I think even I shiver. Watching them together should make me jealous, shouldn't it? I should want to be the one she's flirting with and kissing, but it's not like that.

I don't want to replace Raphael at her side. I want to join him.

What a fucking mess.

"Leave me alone!"

The three of us turn, our gazes directed off in the distance toward the flower bushes as we try to find the source of that shout.

Hayliel is the first to react, jumping to her feet and heading into the darkness. Raphael and I follow close behind, the three of us approaching slowly, speeding up only after we hear a thump and a soft whimper.

As my eyes adjust, I can make out four figures in the dark. Three of them hover over the fourth angel, who's huddled on the ground while they take turns kicking. My blood boils.

"What the fuck do you think you're doing?" Hayliel demands.

At the sound of our approach, the three assholes stop their attack and turn to us.

"Ah, if it isn't the demon. Out at night to hunt your prey, are you?" the tallest one says with a smirk.

I recognize him from history class. Cadriel, I think. He's the dick-cheese who made some comment about Hayliel turning into a demon.

Before Raphael and I can come to her defense, she responds. Her smile turns sinister beneath the pale light of the moon.

"Can you really call it a hunt if the prey is so easy to catch? It looks like I've found my next meal fairly easily, and it's a full course." Her gaze travels between the guys as she walks toward them on slow, even steps — a true predator before pouncing.

In a flash, she rushes Cadriel, opening her mouth wide like she's going to sink her teeth into his flesh. I swear to the Archangels, he might have pissed his pants.

He jumps back, knocking one of his friends to the ground as he tries to get away.

Damn. It's a genius idea to use their own accusations and taunts against them. They look fucking terrified. And maybe, if they truly think she is what they say she is, they'll leave her the hell alone.

Her laugh echoes through the clearing as the three assholes scramble to get as far away as possible.

"It won't be over." Hayliel sighs. "It never is."

The angel on the ground sits up. He's actually quite tall now that he's not huddled into a ball. He doesn't look that reassured either, since his pupils are wide against thin, brown irises. He can't truly believe she's a demon, right?

After another step forward, Hayliel crouches down so that she's at eye level with our new buddy. The closer she gets, though, the more distance he tries to put between them.

"Dude, I'm not a demon. And even if I were, I'd rather inhale a week-old taco-Tuesday fart than put my mouth anywhere near that guy. Doesn't mean I won't use their fear and bullshit to my advantage. Are you alright?"

Raphael and I can't help but laugh because, damn, she's not wrong. Not exactly sure I'd go that far, but still.

The angel tries to hold back his own chuckle, but finally gives in and lets one loose, taking her outstretched hand.

"Nothing that won't heal. Thanks for scaring them away. You're great at the whole hungry-demon thing." It's barely no-ticeable beneath the pale glow of the night sky, but I'm pretty sure he's blushing.

"Even you could be scary, uh..."

"Gagiel. My name is Gagiel."

Raphael laughs, but quickly covers it with a cough. "Allergies," he says when the three of us look at him.

Allergies my fucking ass. That's only something mortals have to deal with, not us. Instead of saying anything, though, Hayliel goes back to her conversation.

"Right. Even you could be scary, Gagiel, but they need to believe it. For me, that's easy. More than half the school believes I've actually spawned from some demon overlord. Here"—she quickly taps what I assume is her number into his slate—"If they bother you again, come find me."

He stares at her almost reverently, like she's a long-lost deity instead of the vicious beast people pretend she is. "Thank you. I-I will."

Hayliel nods, stepping back. "Which house are you in?"

Before Gagiel can respond, I chime in. "He's at Knowledge house with me."

Her determined gaze flashes to mine. "Think you could make sure he gets back to his room safely? I don't trust Cadriel and his squad of dildos not to cause more shit."

I nod, which earns me a big smile from Hayliel that warms my insides. She's like a firefly, lighting up the darkness.

Turning to Gagiel, she says, "This is my friend Theo. I trust him with my life, and he'll get you home safely."

"Thank you again, Hayliel. I'm sorry everyone misjudges you."

We part ways, and as Gagiel and I take flight, I hear Raphael offer to help clean up our mess at the bonfire and fly her home.

"She's really nice," he says when we're halfway back.

"She is. Deserves far more credit than she gets."

"Well, she has every ounce of my respect. No one's ever stood in harm's way to help me before. If she had been here last year, maybe there wouldn't have been so many dropouts."

We hover above Knowledge house as I take in his words. "Wait. You're a second year?"

"Yeah ... the rest of my friends applied for virtual learning after some senior wouldn't leave us alone. I bet if they knew someone like her was here, they'd come back."

What's with these angels who can't just leave others alone? How messed up of a childhood did you have to have in order to treat others so poorly? It baffles me. And for those angels to have been bullied so much that they physically fucking left blows my fucking mind. The audacity of bullies, I swear.

"She's pretty incredible, and I know she means what she told you. She's got your back, and I do too. Take my number as well, just in case. Think you can get back to your room alright?"

"Yes. Thanks for everything. I won't forget it."

"No worries, man."

I watch as he flies off toward the back of the house, far happier than he'd been when we first saw him.

There's something about Hayliel that just makes everyone feel better. She's kind and forgiving, and downright protective.

Regardless of how much she's bullied, it doesn't stop her from putting herself in the firing line to protect someone else.

Like a guardian, I'll stand at her side as she makes this world a better place. And while she's protecting the underdogs, I will guard her back with everything I've got.

16

RAPHAEL

Clouds paint the sky a dingy gray, blocking out the light of the sun and setting the campus in a dreary mood. It's hard to believe how much the weather can affect your mental state, but after two days of gray skies, everyone on this damn campus is irritable. Well, everyone except for Hayliel.

I half expect her heart is made of pure sunshine, because even when she's having a bad day, she never snaps or causes a scene. At least, not without reason.

And she's had more than enough reasons lately.

It's been over a week since she and I kissed at the beach. A week of not-so-accidental touches and more sexual tension than anyone should bear in a lifetime, which has undoubtedly led to a week of jerking off while thinking about the feel of her coming apart in my arms.

We haven't been alone since, though not for lack of trying. Class workloads have picked up and become more intense, no doubt the product of our professors wanting to get us ready for midterms and important projects. Between studying, helping Hayliel avoid her tormentors, and keeping an eye on Theo after the now-regular demon attacks, I've barely had a moment to think, let alone figure out how to take the next step with Hayliel. If that's even what she wants.

Archangels know it's what I want, and from the heated glances she sends my way, I think it might be how she feels too. But sometimes I think she looks at Theo the same way, and I wonder if maybe it's all in my head.

Clearly, I'm a mess.

Taking another look in the mirror, I drop my towel and pull on a pair of dark jeans. After another Angelic Powers class with Hayliel where the professor has us moving small objects telekinetically while holding a telepathic conversation, I had to rush back here to find some form of release from the torturous need that always accompanies me when she's around. It's been more of a challenge than I'd care to admit. But how am I to focus on moving random items while I telepathically explain to Hayliel — in great detail, I might add — all the things I plan on doing to her when we're alone? It's madness.

I grab an SCU branded T-shirt from my wardrobe and put it on, wanting to hurry so I can meet Hayliel. She'd messaged

Theo and me in the group chat and said she'd be studying over by the flowers near the arena. Maybe if I'm fast enough, I can steal a few precious moments alone with her.

After I throw a light styling gel into my hair, I grab my slate and notice two missed calls from my parents. Shit. Knowing my mom, she isn't going to give up until I answer, and the longer I go without picking up, the more incensed she'll be.

I call her back, my stomach dropping like it always does when I talk to her.

"Raphael, finally. You know how much I hate when you ignore my calls." Her sharp voice grates on my eardrums, reminding me how grateful I am to be away from home.

"I wasn't ignoring you, Mother. Things are just busy with school."

"Well, yes, dear. I do know that, but Raduriel never missed a call when he attended."

"Of course he didn't, my brother would never dare. Was there a reason for this call, or was it simply a test to see if I'd answer?"

"Don't be so dramatic. And does your mother really need a reason to call? I swear, Raphael. You've always been so difficult, even as a child. I was only calling to check in and see how things were going. Are you enjoying your classes?"

I take a deep, steadying breath and do my best to let go of the defensiveness that always rises to the surface whenever I talk to my parents. That I'm not completely fucked up after years of dodging subtle — and not so subtle — insults truly baffles me. "Classes are great. Most of them are pretty interesting."

"Oh, good. I was worried with your grades not being as high as Raduriel's were that you'd find them too advanced. He did say you can call him if you'd like a tutor. You know he'd be more than happy to help you work through the tough material." Her voice dips in the way it usually does when she compares me to my brother, like I'm a great fool that constantly fails. I guess in her eyes, I always do.

"I appreciate the offer"—*No I don't*—"but I'm managing just fine. I'm late for a study session with my friends, actually, so if there's nothing else?"

"Yes, yes, of course. It's nice to see you so focused on school-work for a change, Raphael. Chat soon!"

I don't bother saying goodbye, or anything else, for that matter. I learned a long time ago that my parents' love comes with strings attached, and eventually I stopped caring. Or, at least, I stopped letting them see I did.

With my bag in hand, I run and jump from my window, falling closer to the ground than I should before snapping my wings open. I'm just so damn *frustrated*. I always feel this way after talking to my mom. Or my brother. My dad too some-times, but at least I can tolerate him in small doses.

I don't fly very far before I spot Hayliel, looking as gorgeous as ever. Then I realize she isn't alone. She's surrounded by three girls, her things tossed around on the ground at her feet. *What the fuck?*

I don't hesitate. With a flap of my wings, I put on a burst of speed before tucking them in and diving to her rescue.

Except I'm too late.

One girl — the leader, I think — shoves Hayliel to the ground. Blood pounds in my ears, my heartbeat thrumming wildly as I land beside the group.

"What the fuck is going on here?" I demand, glaring at the three girls. Immediately, I recognize the leader as Seraphina, the angel who approached me in the cafeteria on the day I met Hayliel. Looks like I made a good choice in avoiding that bitch.

"Nothing that isn't deserved. Just putting the demon-spawn where she belongs. On the ground at our feet." Seraphina smiles like she expects an award for her cruelty. She reaches for me, but I pull my arm away before she can sink her claws in.

I narrow my eyes, red forming at the edges of my vision. "If you ask me, the only *spawn* I see here is you three. Hayliel is better than you'll ever be."

"You can't be—"

"If I ever catch you attacking her again, I promise … you won't like the consequences. Now get the fuck out of here before I do something you'll regret."

The trio of assholes leaves, but not before shooting Hayliel one last glare like this is *her* fault. My chest heaves with the strength it takes not to throttle them, to bury them in the fucking ground for what they've done to my sunshine.

Is it always this bad when Theo and I aren't around? She hasn't mentioned anyone getting physical before.

Shoving those thoughts away, I turn and extend a hand to Hayliel, helping her up from the ground. She's covered in fallen flower petals and dirt, and we both tap away at her clothes to remove it as best we can.

"Are you alright, sunshine?"

"I ... it could have been worse. Honestly, you saved me from smacking them around a bit. Then I really would have been the savage demon-spawn." She smiles, though it doesn't quite reach her eyes. "Thank you for what you said. No one but Dina has ever stood up for me like that before."

I only stare at her, taking in her features. She's almost a foot shorter than me, and as we stand so close, I realize how much I love that she has to tilt her head back to look into my eyes.

I pull another pink flower petal from her hair and cup her cheek as it falls to the ground. "I will never not stand up for you."

Her eyes, locked on mine, flash with heat. I don't think about it, just dip my head and claim her lips. She parts her mouth almost instinctively, like she knows what I want and is more than happy to give it to me. Then she kisses me back, thrusting her tongue against mine until it feels as if I might faint. My cock hardens uncomfortably in my jeans, but I don't care. Not when she's pulling at me as if she can't get enough.

I hoist her up into my arms and she throws her legs around my waist, grinding against my erection. Molten heat spreads through me, making me dizzy. I don't fucking care who sees us. The only thing I care about is the need to be inside her, and I'll fuck her right here if I have to.

A loud buzz crackles around us, but I barely hear it. Hayliel consumes my every thought and movement, matching my passion and fueling the fiery need inside me.

"Attention, students. Please make your way to the arena for a mandatory assembly. Failure to attend may cause immediate expulsion."

The principal's words repeat, echoing from the campus buildings.

Reluctantly, I pull back from Hayliel and press my forehead to hers until our breathing settles. Cock-blocked by a fucking assembly.

Desire pools in her blue eyes, half tempting me to get on my knees right now and find out if I can make her come before the assembly even starts, but I won't risk her scholarship. We'll have plenty of time later to finish what we started.

She places a light kiss on my lips before shimmying down my body to land on her feet. I groan as she slides over my still-hard cock, which only causes her grin to widen further.

"You'll pay for that," I growl, my words heavy with promise. "But first, let's get this over with."

17

HAYLIEL

Raphael helps me pick up the things Seraphina and her little followers tossed around, all the while throwing me heated glances that have my core fluttering with want. Fuck. What I wouldn't give to miss this assembly and spend it with him.

I mean, hell, I should probably thank Seraphina for shoving me since it led to something so passionate, right? I laugh to myself, silently shaking my head. Nah. I don't need to thank that bitch for anything.

Once I've stashed everything back in my bag, Raphael grabs my hand and leads me toward the arena. The area is abuzz with gossip and rumors about what this assembly could be, and I hear more than a few students mention me. A public expulsion. I'm not sure I could handle that.

Raphael must hear it too because he gives my hand a squeeze and doesn't let go, even once the crowds disperse. I spot Theo's mess of curly brown hair on the opposite side of the arena where he sits in an empty row near the end of the bleachers. We head toward that spot, and Raphael finally lets go of my hand to sit on the opposite side of Theo while I take the empty seat at the end.

Their scents mix together until the need to sink my teeth into a chocolate orange has me forgetting where I am. *Now is so not the time, girl.*

It's not long before the arena is full of chattering students, all wanting to know why they've called us here. I receive more than enough stares, spiking my anxiety as I worry that maybe this will be my broadcasted dismissal.

Those thoughts fade away as the principal walks in, followed by several Assassins' Guild members. I quickly recognize one of them is Zeke, wearing the same outfit he wore when we first met, but the others aren't familiar.

The tallest one, a man with thick, chestnut-brown hair, wears a slightly different uniform, making me think he must be an older, more high-ranking member of the Guild. His feathers glint in the late afternoon sun, and that's when I notice the metal tips lining his wings.

My eyes trail back to Zeke, standing perfectly still. He's not looking anywhere in particular, just doing his duty like the others. It's no wonder I've been struggling to tackle him in combat class. His uniform accentuates the broad chest and expansive muscles beneath, reminding me of the powerful way he moves his body.

As if magnetized by my stare, Zeke's eyes fall directly on me. His stoic expression turns sour, and as he shifts his gaze to the angels sitting at my side, his frown deepens.

What an asshole.

I ignore him, looking away and not giving him the satisfaction of my attention. There are far more important matters for me to worry about, anyway. Not to mention I've given him plenty of chances to tell me what the hell crawled up his ass and died, and all he's done is shoot off some bullshit about my Pure friends like I'm not allowed to have any.

When the principal steps forward, the crowd falls silent.

"Thank you all for coming. I regret to inform you that this assembly is of the utmost importance, and I encourage you to pay attention and follow Lieutenant Azrael's direction." He stands back, motioning to the man with steel-tipped wings.

A sigh of relief escapes me. The Assassins' Guild wouldn't be here to escort me off school grounds, not without checking to see if I'd go willingly. So they must be here for something else. But what?

"Good afternoon, fine students of Silver City University. It is with a heavy heart that I stand before you today, but it is of great significance that I do so. If you've been following the news, you'll know that we've seen a recent uptick in demon attacks.

After carefully tracking their movements, we've located what we expect to be their current trajectory, which appears to be this very school."

Shocked gasps and murmurs escape the students around us. There are demons headed here? But why? This is a school with mostly untrained students. What could they possibly gain from coming here? There are far more populated areas in the city if all they want to do is cause harm.

The principal steps forward again and waits three breaths before speaking. "We understand this is jarring news, but please hold your chatter until the end. We have much to get through." When the arena quiets, he steps back again and motions to the Lieutenant.

"Thank you. What Principal Cael says is true. This *is* jarring news. Most of us have not seen this level of demon activity in a very long time. With that being said, the Guild is reinforcing our patrols and doing everything we can to prevent further damage. Until we have fully eliminated the threat, we have decided — with the help and support of the staff here at SCU — to implement a proactive plan. Starting tomorrow, there will be a curfew. All students must return to their dorms by eight p.m. sharp. Anyone caught out beyond that time will face suspension or expulsion, depending. Furthermore, we require that all students stay on campus at all times. There will be no weekend trips to town or to visit family. Consider the school on lockdown."

With so many rules in place, just how much danger are we in? Chatter starts up again from the crowd, but this time the principal doesn't step in to quiet them. Lieutenant Azrael says nothing either, only raises his voice to be heard.

"Finally, we will be adding a self-defense class to the schedule, which will include the steps and procedures to follow if the school falls under attack. These classes are mandatory. Failure to show up may result in expulsion. I want to make something very clear," he says, turning in a circle to survey the students sitting before him. "Do not attempt to fly in the presence of a demon, and avoid being cut with any blade they may carry. Fighting them at all is a last resort, and if at all possible, leave the demon fighting to the professionals. Heed the information I'm sharing with you today and, should the unthinkable occur, you just might survive."

Goosebumps rise on my flesh with his parting words. The school is in lockdown. We have a curfew. And it sounds like there's a very real probability that some of us may not make it out alive. He speaks as if demons attacking the school isn't just a possibility, but a guarantee.

I take in the surrounding students, each one of them looking scared. Some of them even look to me like I'm the reason for these attacks. As if I control the creatures. Fucking assholes.

But Theo is wide eyed and trembling. He looks like he's seen a ghost.

On the other side of him, Raphael notices too, and we share a glance filled with pain and worry for our friend. I have no doubt that he knows more about what's going on than I do, and while I hope they'll share with me one day, today isn't that day.

Raphael talks to Theo in a low tone, whispering things in his ear that I can't hear. I slide closer to him, taking one of his shaking hands in mine and intertwining our fingers. With my other hand, I trace lines on his arm, trying to push as much of my support into him as possible. But as the seconds tick by, it's like he doesn't notice us at all.

He's somewhere far away, and it doesn't seem like either of us can reach him.

18

THEO

Around me, I know the arena sits full of angels, but I don't feel the weight of their presence. I can barely make out their chatter now.

After learning that demons are heading straight for us, I stopped hearing anything at all.

My eyes stay open, staring straight ahead, but I don't see the crowd of people anymore. I no longer breathe in the dust from the arena or feel the seat beneath me. I'm fifteen again, back in that abandoned skatepark where everything changed.

For a second, I swear I can even smell the pale-white flowers blooming on the trees, just like they did back then. But then another scent takes over. One of blood and death.

I don't have to ask where the putrid smell comes from. I already know. That *thing* is killing her, and I do nothing to stop it.

The scene before me plays out, and I watch as a demon tears into the flesh of my childhood friend with ease before plunging a wicked-looking blade into her chest. It's so real, and I wonder for a moment if maybe this time I can save her.

But when the black eyes of the demon turn on me, I freeze.

A deep, jagged scar runs up the side of its face from eyebrow to chin, the milky white clearly visible beneath the blood splatter.

Beyond the beast, my friend lies dead in a pool of her own blood, the dagger no longer stuck in her chest.

She's gone. Brutally murdered. And it's all my fault.

The demon's lips curve up into a smile almost as wicked as the bloodied blade it's holding. A soft buzzing beside me quickly turns into disjointed words and calms my mind despite my looming death, but when I look, there's no one there.

Now there's only six feet between me and the demon. I have nothing to defend myself with, not that I'd even know what to do if I did. But as the demon closes the distance between us, there's a warm tug on my left hand.

Completely ignoring the death blow coming my way, I look down at a small hand wrapped around mine. The words in my ear start to form, coming from a voice I recognize but can't place. Slowly, the arena comes back into focus. I see the students sitting in front of me, deathly quiet as the Assassins' Guild talks of preparedness.

I hear Raphael's quiet words, offering strength and support. Something he's done for me more times than I can count.

And then I see her. Hayliel. She's holding my hand in both of hers, stroking her fingers across my flesh.

Feelings that I've been suppressing for weeks rise to the surface. This girl has been through so much on her own, yet comforts those she cares about. She knows nothing of my past or the reason I'm like this, and yet here she is, helping to ground me. Someday, I want to tell her. I want her to know why I'm this way and share the part of myself that I usually keep hidden.

Her hand is soft, and I'm worried she'll let go before I'm ready. But I have to let her go. Raphael has been upfront with me from the start about his feelings toward her, and I'd never get in the way of his happiness. Or hers.

There are no words I could give them now to show my gratitude, so instead I only offer them each a smile. Raphael knocks his knee against mine, and I expect Hayliel to pull her hand from mine, but she squeezes it instead.

"Are you good?" Raphael whispers, and I nod, not trusting my voice yet.

A prick of unease runs down my spine, and I look up to find one of the Assassins' Guild members scowling at us. Except it's not directed at us at all, I realize. Only Hayliel.

I say nothing, choosing to watch as she glances his way every so often with an odd look on her face. Resignation, perhaps.

Raphael notices too. "Damn, sunshine. I've only seen that guy twice this semester, and both times he's been glaring at you. What the hell is his problem?"

Hayliel ducks her chin and looks down at her hands where they sit wrapped around mine. "Oh. That's my house leader, Zeke. It's nothing. I've come to realize that's just what his face does. Poor guy."

Raphael and I don't respond to her attempt at nonchalance, but we share a look. We'll be keeping an eye on him.

The assembly ends, and the principal sends us off with a reminder of the upcoming curfew. Neither one of us moves yet, content to skip the crowd as they rush to exit the arena.

Raphael leans forward so he can see us both. "I don't know about you two, but I'd like to escape all the doom and gloom for a little while, at least before the rules set in. Why don't we head to the Knowledge library and see if we can find anything to help your wing search?"

Hayliel beams at him, and I can't help but watch her excitement as she agrees. She turns to me then, her gaze open and questioning, like she's not sure I'll be interested.

Internally, I let out a sigh of relief that she doesn't seem to realize just how far I'd go to make her happy. That's a secret only for me. One I'll keep buried deep inside, far away from Raphael and Hayliel. They'll make each other happy, I know it.

"I think that's the perfect way to spend our last night before curfew. Raph, why don't you take her and I'll catch up in a few. I have to stop at my room first."

He eyes me skeptically, but I ignore it. I really do need to grab my slate, but most of all, I just want a moment alone to compose myself. Raphael has helped me work through my flashbacks before. Countless times, really. So I know he's aware of my routine. I need to shower and rinse away the sweat and images still lingering in my mind.

"You'll be okay alone?" Hayliel asks with another squeeze of my hand. "We could come with you for support, if you'd like? I promise not to snoop through your things ... Too much, anyway." She smiles, and my chest tightens.

"I'll be fine. But I'd like you to ask me that again next time."

"Deal."

She stands then, letting go of my hand and the chill burrows into my bones immediately. For a second, she only watches the crowd of students gingerly making their way toward the small exit on the other side of the arena.

"What are you doing?" Raphael asks her.

In a flash, her gray wings burst free of her back and she spreads them wide. "I swear, those fools would lose their wings if they weren't attached. Let's get out of here."

She reaches out a hand to both of us then, and we take it, letting our own wings free. With a push off the bleachers, we're in the air, soaring above the crowd of students who stop and stare at us as we make our way toward Knowledge house. Hayliel laughs, the sound catching on the wind and seeming to wrap around my very being.

How does she manage such happiness in the face of everything that's happened to her? I could learn a thing or two from it, I think.

It's harder to unclasp her hand from mine than I care to admit, but I do so anyway and head toward my balcony. Tapping my wing against the sensor, the door unlocks and I enter the room with an audible sigh. I waste no time jumping in the shower and washing away the grime and dirt from my body, forcing the memories with it.

Once I'm dressed, I grab my slate, noticing that it's only been fifteen minutes since I left them, and head out the door and down the stairs.

Surprise hits me when I find them waiting there instead of in the library.

"What's going on?" I ask, worry thick in my voice.

Raphael stands from where he was leaning against the wall. "I think this one has an edging kink. She insisted we stay here and wait."

With a laugh, Hayliel smacks him lightly on the arm. "It wouldn't have been the same if you weren't here. But now that you are ... can we go?"

Her excitement is infectious as we walk down the hall toward the massive library doors gilded in silver, gold, and black.

"Holy shit," Hayliel says, rubbing a hand along the molding.

As if on cue, Raphael and I each grab a handle and tug. The doors open to reveal rows upon rows of shelving and books, with ladders on tracks and large areas meant for collaborating with peers. Even I can admit it's impressive. I try to come here every morning before breakfast and sometimes in the evening too, but I've barely scratched the surface of what's inside.

"Guys ... am I drooling? I think I'm drooling."

Raphael moves a hand to Hayliel's chin, then feigns disgust while he wipes his hand on his pants. Her eyes widen until she catches the smirk on his face.

"Ha-ha," she replies, before focusing her attention back on the library. "Where do we even start?"

I know a few sections that might hold what we need, so I tell them to find a spot for us to sit and head over to grab a few books. I end up bringing an entire fucking cart back, loaded with books mostly on our history. If we can't find something in here, we'll read up on anatomy or power. Fuck, I'll read a damn book on feathers if it helps her find answers.

We share a couch as we read. Raphael sits on one end and I on the other with Hayliel in between. The cushions are so deep that she can't sit properly on them. At six foot three, I have no issues touching my own feet to the floor.

This couch is rather cozy, if I'm honest. But it's cute to watch her try to find a comfortable position. She ends up pulling the coffee table closer, shaking off her shoes, and propping her sock-clad feet on it. I do my best to focus on the words inside my book instead of the warmth of her thigh against mine while she sits sprawled out with a pillow on her lap.

I shouldn't be noticing these things. Not while knowing how my best friend feels. His friendship means more to me than anything, including the budding feelings I have for this gray-winged angel that seem to grow with each passing second. He's a far better option for her, anyway. At least he's normal.

My damage would only drag her down.

We make it through half the stack of books without a single helpful clue. These books are in too good a condition to be anything but rewrites, likely put together after the Archangels took over. It hurts to watch Hayliel's excitement turn to defeat, but Raph and I try to reassure her that there is so much more to learn, and we'd be more than happy to help her.

Her slate pings a short while later. She stands, stretching. "I have to go meet Dina. Can you show me where to put these?"

"Leave them. We'll take care of it." My chest caves in a little. I'm not ready for her to leave just yet, or Raphael, even. I know myself enough to guess that I won't be getting much sleep tonight. The nightmares will claim it from me.

She bends down to put her sneakers back on. "Are you sure?"

"Positive. We'll walk through the stacks next time, though, deal?"

"I'll hold you to that. Thanks for today. And if what they said really is true, please be safe."

"Fly straight home, sunshine," Raphael calls to her as she heads toward the exit.

With her gone, we fall into silence, either caught up in the texts or our own thoughts. I slam another book shut, annoyed not to have found anything that could help her. Raphael does the same, placing his own on the table before grabbing a new one off the shelf, but he doesn't open it.

"We'll find something eventually, Theo. It's clear we both have feelings for her. It's not like either of us will give up until she finds what she's looking for."

My breath stutters as I take in his words. He doesn't sound upset or worried. He says the words like my hidden feelings are an obvious fact more than anything else. Even so, I can't help but worry.

"Raph, I didn't ... I wouldn't ..."

"Theo, it's fine. Hayliel is special. It would take a fool not to fall head over heels for her."

I grab another book off the cart instead of responding. What would I even say? There's no denying it now. He clearly knows me better than I expected, though I'm not exactly certain why I doubted him in the first place.

Raphael doesn't push the subject. He opens his own book, skimming the table of contents before flipping ahead. I try to concentrate on my own research, but I can't move forward until I get this off my chest.

"You're right. I have developed feelings for her. But I would never act on them. This isn't some sort of competition between us to see who she picks. You've been into her from the very start and I just want you both to be happy," I tell him, knowing full well she wouldn't be happy with me. Maybe in the beginning. But my baggage is too heavy, and it wouldn't take long to drag us both down.

"Maybe she wouldn't have to choose. After everything I've seen from her since school started, it's clear she's not a prude. Fuck, I've seen the way she looks at you, Theo. Maybe she'd accept us both."

I stop halfway through flipping a page. *Maybe she wouldn't have to choose.* It's not unheard of for angels to date multiple people at once, but most of those are all Pure relationships. Hayliel is battling enough disdain from the other students already. If she started dating multiple people, wouldn't that just cause more shit?

"I dunno ..." is all I manage to say because I close my eyes, trying to picture what Raphael suggests. We look happy, sharing her, but then I see a fissure form between me and them, one brought on by my episodes and regular distracted behavior. In the end, my baggage would only force her to choose, anyway.

"We don't have to do anything yet. Archangels know there's enough shit going on right now for us to be worrying about how she'll take the suggestion, but I want you to know it's on the table. There isn't an angel alive that I'd rather share her with."

"If she even agrees to it."

Raphael nods. "If she even agrees."

We both turn back to our books, but my mind is racing a million miles a minute. Suddenly, I think of the angel that glared at her during the assembly. Her house leader, Zeke.

Something tells me he'd want a say in our sharing her too.

The weekend passes by in a blur of confusion and panic as the reality of our situation sinks in. Students huddle inside the library and common rooms, not bothering to venture outside like usual. Everyone is on edge, waiting for an attack to come wipe us out, and there's safety in numbers, I suppose.

The impending doom doesn't mean we get a break from classes, much to everyone's dismay. Nor does it mean Harold the Herald takes a break from his weekly news report.

I eye the stack of papers piled at the entryway with a grimace.

After last week's release chewed me up and spat me out, I almost don't want to read it. With the curfew, I've had to spend more and more time away from my friends. Dina is here, of course, and she does her best to protect and support me, but I can't expect her to stay with me twenty-four seven.

She might not be on a scholarship like I am, but her father has pretty damn high expectations of her. He's a well-respected Pure with a Fallen daughter, and as much as he cherishes her in the public eye, behind closed doors he expects nothing but perfection. It hasn't always been like this, but I guess he's been more on edge lately with the demons swarming around the city and can't handle any misstep, even from his daughter.

It's hard to watch her struggle under the weight of his expectations.

Given all that, I can't fault her for putting her studies first, even if I think she should relax too. She constantly supports me, so doing the same for her is the least I can do.

A few students rush to grab the newest edition of the *SCU Weekly Observer* and I cave, snagging a copy of my own before running up the stairs to my room. If something in this damn newsletter triggers me, I'll have to deal with it alone, and I'd rather be safe in the confines of my bedroom than under a microscope in the common room. Bullies only want a reaction, and there's no way in fucking hell I'll give them one.

Once I shut the door, I head toward the bed and curl up to read.

Facing Demon Forces: Is There a Spy in Our Midst?
By Harold the Herald

Rising demon attacks have forced the students of Silver City University into a lockdown after the Assassins' Guild expressed concerns. It would appear the creatures are becoming bolder, attacking more frequently, and, as is their assumption, heading directly for the school.

The students I spoke to on this matter sounded anxious and scared, but more than one brought up a rather unmistakable coincidence. Temperance Sweeney, a long-time friend of Seraphina Beckett, was the first to notice the shocking correlation. "I'm not the only one who thinks it's strange that the demons have upped their attacks at the same moment Hayliel arrived here. They've never shown an interest in this glorious school before now, so one has to wonder if all they want is their beloved spawn back. Perhaps if we handed her over to them, they'd back off."

Strong assumptions from Miss Temperance, but one can't ignore the possibility altogether. Perhaps there is a connection the authorities should dig into, but that is not for me to say. Several other students agreed with Temperance, including Cadriel Hammerman, who shared a frightening personal interaction with the gray-winged student. "She attacked me and my friends at night, lunging for us from the shadows, and I barely escaped. It was like she blended in with the darkness, camouflaging herself like I've heard demons can. Authorities have warned we have a demon attack forthcoming, but I'm afraid it's already started."

In a rather unusual turn of events, I spoke with second-year student Gagiel Nisbet, who had an entirely different account of events. "Cadriel is as much of a cad as his name states. He

and his friends were assaulting me, and Hayliel saved me from their wrath. She's not a demon or anything else nefarious. Hayliel Gracelin is one of the kindest angels I know, and Silver City University is a far greater place with her in it."
So, whose story is true? Are her gray wings only a defect, or are they the sign that demon blood runs through her veins? Unfortunately, even I don't have that answer. But I, along with all of you, look forward to finding out.

Despite the cruel words from Temperance and Cadriel, I can't stop my lips from tilting upward in a smile. It's no surprise that Temperance would try to get rid of me. She and Seraphina have been against my being here from the very start. And I knew Cadriel wouldn't be able to keep his mouth shut about what transpired last week. Their comments I expected.

But Gagiel ... his words catch me off guard and light a fire inside me I can't ignore. Words and actions matter, and while I can't do anything about my own circumstances, I can at least help others.

A knock on my balcony door has my head jerking at the unexpected noise. I barely use that entrance myself, though I really should make more of an effort to. Any chance to avoid the wary gazes of my housemates. Another knock reverberates through the door, and I consider ignoring it, hoping whoever's out there will give up and leave, but then my slate pings.

Raphael: It's only us, not a stalker.

I laugh and race to the door, throwing it open with a grin plastered on my face as my two friends bound inside.

"Wasn't sure if you were going to open the door, sunshine," Raphael says with a laugh.

"I definitely considered ignoring it, but you texted, so."

Theo heads further into my room, taking a seat on the sofa chair. "Worried it might be your grumpy house captain?"

"Archangels, no. He wouldn't approach me even if I were on fire and he held a hose." The words are a joke, but I can't help the sting they cause. Theo looks like he's going to say more, but he's interrupted before he can.

"Hayliel, Hayliel, Hayliel. Did you really lock yourself in here to read this trash?" Raphael holds up the newsletter I'd left lying on my bed, the look on his face reminding me of a scolding parent. It's kind of adorable.

"This one actually isn't too bad. Seems our new friend Gagiel had a few words to say." I watch as my two friends huddle over the paper, scoffing at the mention of Temperance and Cadriel and smiling when they reach the end.

"This deserves a celebration! We were already coming to whisk you away to the beach, but now we have a reason to drink this bottle of wine I snagged from the staff fridge."

"How did you ... actually, no. I don't want to know." It's only then I notice the swim trunks they wear, and the towels draped around their necks. How the hell could I have missed those?

Raphael opens my closet, spying the new bathing suit Dina bought me as a welcome gift. She called it a one-piece, but I think a bikini has more coverage. "Here. Put this on, and then we'll head out."

He tosses it to me, and I'm seconds away from putting it back when I stop myself. Would it really be so bad if I wore this? It's only Raphael and Theo with me, after all. I walk to the bathroom, determination pushing me forward as I change into the incredibly revealing bathing suit.

With a glance in the mirror, heat rises to my cheeks and my nipples pebble at the slight chill in the air. Or maybe it's the thought of what the boys on the other side of the door will think when they see me. I check the back once more, making sure my ass isn't hanging out too far, and then open the door.

Raphael whistles low, biting his fist as if to stop himself from doing anything else. I watch as Theo swallows hard, the muscles of his jaw working like he desperately wants to say something but holds himself back. I can't help the zing of triumph that flits through my body.

I grab a tank top and pair of shorts from my closet, pulling those on over my bathing suit before looking at the two attractive angels in my room. "I'm ready," I say, my voice coming out more breathless than I intended.

A few students mingle near the fountain or the fire pit as we fly the short distance from Fallen house to the beach. Luckily, when we land on the wooden dock, it's only the three of us.

I glance at the spot where Raphael and I had our picnic, my stomach fluttering at the memories.

"Are you coming?" Raphael asks, and the smirk on his handsome face tells me he knows exactly where my mind just went. From the heat in his gaze, I bet his thoughts were there too.

Instead of answering, I run down the dock, ripping my clothes off as I go and tossing them behind me. When the guys notice what I'm doing, they rush to follow until we're all racing toward the water. Raphael jumps in first, followed by Theo, and then me. I blame their damn long-ass legs.

The water isn't frigid, exactly, but it isn't warm either. The air tastes of fresh salt and driftwood, reminding me of the one time my family visited a beach when I was younger. We'd joined Dina and her family on a weekend trip to the coast and had the most magical time. But that was before her father knew of my unique trait.

Not allowing myself to linger on such sad thoughts, I tread water and focus on Raphael and Theo where they wrestle amidst the waves. Raphael pushes Theo beneath the surface, the ocean mirroring the blue of his irises and making my breath catch. Suddenly, Theo breaks free and forces Raphael down, holding him under with muscles far more prominent than I expected to see from his lanky frame.

Desire pools low in my belly, but I shake it off. These are my friends, not my boyfriends, so I shouldn't be ogling them with such desperation. When Raphael finally pops up, I whip around in a circle, splashing both of them before diving beneath the surface and swimming away.

Things are different now, and while I may not be able to fully ignore the lustful thoughts racing through my mind, these two angels accept me for every ounce of who I am.

Why shouldn't I have a little fun?

Hours later, I land on my balcony mere seconds before the curfew deadline. Despite the sand that covers my legs, I couldn't have had a better day. Happiness bubbles up inside me as I press my wings to the small sensor. Only when I move to open the door, it doesn't budge. What the fuck?

I try again, giving the task my full attention, but still the door doesn't unlock. An error code flashes across the screen three times before disappearing. The number means absolutely nothing to me, and my breath hitches as panic settles in my gut.

I send a quick message to the group chat with Raphael and Theo, fumbling over the letters with my shaking hands.

Raphael: Shit. We programmed our wings to your sensor while you were changing.

Theo: Not for any creepy reason, just in case of emergencies.

A laugh escapes me, though it sounds more hysterical and crazed than anything else. I like the idea of them having access to my dorm. I only wish I'd known this before curfew.

Raphael: I'll head over now. Maybe mine will still work.

Hayliel: Don't be silly. It's past curfew. I'll just use my key.

Theo: Let us know when you're safely inside.

I smile despite the shitty situation. The guys are always looking out for me. From day one, I knew I could count on those two. I only hope my outcast status doesn't make things harder for them.

Flying down from the balcony, I make my way to the front door of Fallen house and slip inside. Students eye me as I walk past the common room in my wet shorts and tank top, leaving little granules of sand in my wake. It could be worse, though. At least I have my bathing suit covered.

When I make it to my door, I sigh a breath of relief. Home sweet home. *Once I'm inside, I can fix the balcony sensor. It's all good. I still have my key.*

Except I don't. I dig through the pockets of my shorts, pulling them inside out to reveal nothing but sand. But where ...

Fuck. I hadn't bothered to bring my key because I'd been dead set on using the balcony. Shit!

Crossing the hall to Dina's room, I knock on her door. It's fine. She'll let me inside, and I'll just crash with her tonight until I can figure it out. No big deal.

Except it is a big fucking deal. Dina doesn't answer, and pressing my ear to the door only proves my assumption that she's not even in her room.

My heart pounds as I try to think of another solution. Theo and Raphael can't come without breaking curfew, and I won't risk their spot here. But that also means that I can't go to them without facing the same consequences. What the hell am I supposed to do?

A memory flashes through my mind of my first day. Of Zeke walking me to my room and unlocking the door with a master key. What had he said? *"If you ever lose it or have trouble accessing your room, come find me."*

Fucking shit.

I don't even have his number or email programmed into my slate. Why hadn't I at least taken his email from the welcome packet? I'm an idiot.

With a few deep breaths, I make my way up the stairs toward the eighth floor. Resolve settles inside me as I stand in front of his door. He's the Fallen house leader. It's not as if he can turn me away, right?

I rap my knuckles on his door twice before stepping back to wait. And wait. By the time I count to sixty, my worry turns to frustration. Seriously? What could he possibly be doing in there?

Stepping closer, I press my ear to the door, listening for any signs of life inside.

Nothing.

I try again, this time cupping my hand to my ear where it presses against the solid wood.

The door flies open, my hand falling to land on Zeke's bare chest where he stands inside the threshold.

Mortification freezes my every limb, including the one currently plastered to his pec. With dark-green SCU sweatpants riding low on his hips, I try to ignore the outline of his dick, but it's almost impossible.

He doesn't pull away, only tilts his head in question as his gaze travels along my sandy clothes. "Can I help you?"

His words jolt me out of my humiliation, and I pull my hand back. "Uh, sorry. Yes. I need you, master." *By the Archangels. Try again, Hayliel.* "Your master key, I mean. I'm locked out of my room."

He smirks, amused at my stuttering. I can hardly concentrate when he stands there looking so fucking hot. Christ. This is why women let hot guys treat them like shit. It's like our brains stop functioning properly in their presence.

"Why don't you just enter through the balcony?"

"I tried, but it kept giving me an error. That's when I realized I'd left my key inside."

He sighs, walking to his desk to grab the key before heading back to the door. "Let's go."

"You aren't going to put a shirt on?"

"No. Will that be a problem for you, hummingbird?"

I bite my lip and shake my head, not trusting myself to speak.

He takes the lead, with me following behind him as we head toward my room. I take the time to study his broad frame. A tattoo runs along his spinal cord, stretching across his shoulders and down the backs of his arms. I remember this from the start-of-term party but, between the neon paint and our tryst, I didn't have time to study it then.

The skeletal design is gorgeous, if not slightly haunting. Part of me wants to ask him if it holds some deeper meaning, but I don't actually think he'd answer me. He's only unlocking my dorm room because it's his job as house leader. Nothing more.

To my surprise, he doesn't just unlock the door and leave. Instead, he rests his hands against the top of the door frame, watching as I place my slate down and slip off my sandals.

"Can you show me that error? It's rare that these machines act up, but it isn't unheard of."

"Of course, come on in."

He follows me to the balcony door, which I prop open with my laundry hamper. Probably should have checked that I hadn't laid my panties on top when I changed earlier, but it's too late now.

After placing my wing on the sensor, Zeke reads the error that flashes across the screen before turning to me. "Have you done anything different to this recently?"

"Not personally, but two of my friends calibrated their wings to it earlier today. Could that have caused the issue?" At my words, Zeke's expression changes entirely. His smirk turns into a frown, his eyes narrowing on me as if he knows exactly which friends I'm referring to.

Fuck. Maybe I should have just lied.

"I'm not sure who taught you about safety, or if you've been paying attention to the dangers around us lately, but I'd advise against letting every Raphael, Theo, and Hubert have access to your room."

"That's not—"

"They only built these systems to hold two sets of wings. Yours and one other angel, if you so choose. Unfortunately for you, it seems you'll have to pick the one you want the most." He turns back to the sensor and holds down a button along the side, before tapping in a code. He works too quickly for me to decipher what he did, and before I know it, he's let his wings out and stands at the edge of my balcony. "I've reset the device. All you need to do is scan your wings and it should work. Don't lose your keys again, hummingbird. I may not be so available to you the next time."

And with that, he jumps from the ledge.

Leave it to Zeke to ruin my good fucking day.

20

HAYLIEL

Despite the new rules and protection, no demons have attacked the school.

Reports still come in regularly detailing other attacks off school grounds, but none have dared come too close. Because of that, the students have gotten bolder. They spend more time outside of their dorms after classes, staying out as long as they can until curfew.

I've even heard mutterings of a secret late-night party in the woods tonight. In their usual style, I haven't received an invite, but that's alright. It's not as if I'd risk my spot here to hang out with people that don't like me, anyway.

I can't help but hope the lack of activity means the demons won't come at all. I've spoken with my parents almost daily since the assembly. Even though my area is a more likely target zone than where they are, I'm still worried something will happen to them. As much as they might try to fool me into thinking they're happy in their new home, I see through the bullshit. The outskirts of town are a far cry from the life we used to live. I wish I could visit them. But with the university on lockdown, I can't leave.

The desire to yawn seeps through me so suddenly that I can't hold it back. Last night I stayed up far later than I intended, working on perfecting my telekinesis abilities. I still have a lot of work to do, but it's gotten a little easier, even if my brain is fried today because of it.

Plus, if I hadn't stayed up so late, I never would have caught Zeke flying home in the middle of the night. It was too dark to see if he wore his Guild uniform or not, and though that was most likely the case, I hadn't been able to stop the images of him with another angel. Had I caught him breaking curfew and doing the fly of shame back to his dorm? Not that I should care. Most of the time he ignores me, and the rest of the time he only scowls at me so deeply I'm worried his face will stay like that.

Glancing at my slate, I stifle a groan at the time. I sit in my last class of the day: Chronicles of Silver City. The content itself I find quite interesting, but I don't have a single friend among the other students in this class, and the professor seems more than happy to let things play out if they don't interfere with her lectures.

Last week, we read about the dreaded God who used to rule the city hundreds of years ago before the Archangels overthrew him. Afterward, we were told to write a one-page essay about why we thought God acted the way he did. It felt like a silly assignment, though I completed it anyway. How am I supposed to know why God did what he did? I had never met him. In fact, there aren't many angels left who were alive when he ruled.

"We previously learned about the deplorable things God did to the angel race, and this week we'll discuss our saviors. The ruling Archangels. If you'll recall, the Archangels once served God in all things. They would help him rule the angels, watch over the people of Earth, and protect both from demons. They did so without a single complaint. But when God's desires turned dark, they knew they had to strike before all of angelkind disappeared for good."

I read through the text on my slate, wondering how much of it is true and how much of it is only posturing to make the Archangels look good. Had God truly become evil? And if he did, then what made him change? It shocked me that no one seemed to care about that minor detail.

"It is said that God wanted to rid the world of our Fallen brethren. He conspired to create a world where only the Pure could survive beneath him. For, you see, he sensed a change in the air. One which warned of the Archangels' strength, and he wanted no other being to match his power."

A hand goes up from a girl in the middle of the class, and I recognize the bracelet she wears almost instantly. One of Seraphina's little minions.

"Go ahead," Professor Sofiel says, her red-painted lips curved into a smile that looks anything but inviting.

"What do you think God would have done to a gray-winged angel?" she asks, and the class snickers. My ears turn hot as I feel several pairs of eyes turn to look at me, but I ignore them.

"That's enough, students. Fantastic question, Temperance. Given what we know of God's will in his final days, I believe he would have eradicated that being, along with any other non-Pure angel."

This only causes the class to burst into laughter once more. I sit there in utter shock. How could a professor even say those things, especially with me sitting in her class? Does she not care at all what that implies?

"Quiet, now. As I was saying. The Archangels devised a plan to overthrow God and save us. They worked tirelessly and in secret, trusting only themselves and a few Pure angels to ensure nothing of the plan would get back to God before they could secure it. Despite the Archangels' efforts, they lost many that day. God's might was powerful, but in the end, it was no match for the joined forces of the Archangels. For the duration of class, I'd like you to finish reading chapter five and complete the questions at the end of the chapter."

I give the assignment my utmost attention, if only to ignore the whispers. At least their cruel words serve me in some way.

I'll finish these questions before class is over and won't have to work on them tonight.

The rest of the period passes quickly, and I'm finishing up the last question just as class ends.

I don't bother standing, choosing to wait until everyone leaves before exiting myself. They've tripped me enough times for me to learn a little self-preservation.

The class is almost empty by the time I pack up my things, but a few students still mill about. Someone stands at the front of the class, talking animatedly with the professor while Temperance approaches me.

"How does it feel to know that even God would have gotten rid of you? The great creator himself would have deemed you dangerous. Maybe once the Archangels learn of you, they'll come to remove you themselves." Her voice is sweet, almost charming. A perfect contrast to the venomous words escaping her lips.

"If I truly am spawned from demons, shouldn't you be worried? From what I hear, they can easily rip an angel apart with their bare hands." I stare down at my fingers, flexing them before jabbing my hand forward. She jumps back, though I wasn't even close to touching her.

"G-get away from me."

Grabbing a piece of paper and pen from my bag, I draw a random shape with thick black lines, like the one I saw in Zeke's research last week, while spewing gibberish. I have no problems playing the demonic creature everyone thinks I am.

Temperance hasn't moved, but her eyes have turned from stuck-up bitch to wary bitch as I put the last touches on the symbol and toss the paper at her. She jumps back to avoid any piece of it touching her, but still she doesn't leave.

It's time to have a little fun.

With jerky movements, I contort my body at weird angles, letting creepy sucking sounds escape my throat before I lurch toward her.

She damn near trips over a desk on her way out of the classroom.

A little shot of victory shoots through me, even if that might not have been my smartest move. But what am I supposed to do? Their tormenting hasn't stopped. It hasn't lessened either. So maybe if I lean in to it a little, they'll leave me alone.

As the adrenaline eases from my body, I realize how fried my nerves are. Midterms are fast approaching, and classes are only getting harder. It doesn't help that this school is filled with assholes, so I rarely get a break from their bullshit. Even Zeke, who appears to be my now-constant partner in combat, hasn't taken the stick out of his ass. The only bright spots in my life are my three friends. I spend as much time with them as possible outside of classes. The curfew hasn't helped, but Dina and I spend most of our evenings studying together in one of our rooms.

Raphael has agreed to help me study for our Angelic Powers midterm today. I had hoped the disadvantages of growing up with two Fallen parents wouldn't hinder my progress here, but it appears I was wrong. I've gotten the hang of telepathy, at least with him, but it's doing that with the telekinesis bit that I'm struggling with.

To be honest, I've always had a hard time focusing on two things at once, so it's no surprise I need a little extra tutoring in this area. Though, I'm questioning if maybe I should have requested someone else's help for this. I have a feeling Raphael is going to be too distracting a tutor.

Once I'm back in my room, I change out of the school uniform and into some sweatpants, paired with a plain gray tank top and SCU zip-up hoodie. If I'm going to melt my brain by studying all afternoon, I may as well be comfortable.

Raphael asked me to meet him by the statues near his house since we'll be studying in his room. Theo was original-ly supposed to join us, but the news of another demon attack left him preoccupied and withdrawn. We tried to convince him it would be a good way to keep his mind off it, but he said he'd rather see if he could learn anything helpful instead of worrying about school. Not that he has much to worry about. That guy is already far smarter than I am.

With him busy, that leaves Raphael and me alone. It feels too weird to ask him to change study locations now that it's just the two of us. Part of me is grateful that we won't have an audience. I get shit on by the other students enough that I really don't want them to know how hard I'm struggling. But the other part of me wonders if being alone with him is such a good idea.

I find him standing near the angel statue in a near identical pose, and I can't help but laugh.

"Anyone ever tell you that you look like him?" I ask as I land on my feet.

"You'd be the first, though I haven't exactly posed for any-one else. Besides, I'm pretty sure my wingspan is bigger." In a flash, his wings are out and spread wide, just like the statue.

Well shit, he might be right, though I'll never tell him that. His wings are beautiful, appearing both bright and colorless at the same time. The sun reflects off the white feathers until they almost shimmer like a thousand diamonds. It's hard to look away from.

"Do you like what you see, sunshine?" he asks, his voice teasing and abruptly shaking me out of my daze.

"Wouldn't you like to know?" I reply with a wink before walking past him toward the house of Power.

I only get so far before he calls out, "Come on, let's fly in-stead." He holds out his hand, and I take it without hesitation.

We fly around the building toward a balcony that faces the trees. It's really quite stunning from up here, almost like a private forest just for him.

Using his wing, he unlocks his door before turning to ges-ture me inside. His room is a similar size to mine, though he's on a lower floor than I am. Likely because of the sheer number of Pure students that attend SCU, but it wouldn't surprise me if the Fallen dorms were just smaller. We are Fallen, after all.

There's a large, king-sized bed in the corner. It's low to the ground, which is odd to see compared to how high my bed is. But maybe this is what all the dorms are like here. On the opposite side of the room sit two leather barrel chairs. The navy coloring matches well with the other accents within the room.

It's neater than I expected, but more like my room. *Messier than Zeke's*, I think. I instantly regret that thought, and hope Raphael can't read any of it on my face. Who the hell compares guys' bedrooms, anyway? Only fucking weirdos, apparently.

I bring my things to one of the navy chairs before sitting and rummaging through my bag to find my slate. My hands are clammy when I pull it out and set it on the table. I fidget with my shirt, looking everywhere but at Raphael as he sits in the chair across from me.

"You're nervous. Why?"

I bury my face in my hands. "What if I can't figure it out? Fuck, Raphael. What if I fail and they kick me out?"

He's in front of me instantly, kneeling on the floor at my feet and lightly moving my hands away so he can see my face.

"Hey. You aren't going to fail because I won't let you. You'll get the hang of it, I promise. Do you trust me?" he asks, his voice full of sincerity.

And I'm nodding just like the very first time he asked, before I even realize it. I'm no longer shocked at how easy it is for me to answer that question. Despite having known him for only a short time, I trust Raphael completely. He's had my back on more than one occasion, and I truly believe he'll give up every hour of sleep to keep me here.

"Good. Remember that trust in a moment." He leans in to press a quick kiss to my lips before darting back to the chair opposite mine.

His kiss distracts me from his words, but once the fog fades away, unease spreads through my limbs.

"Raph ... What do you have planned?"

He goes utterly still for a moment, and the oddest look crosses his face. Surprise mixed with happiness, perhaps? Whatever it is, he shakes it off quickly and says, "Nothing you won't like, eventually." He throws me a wink before pulling out a pen from his bag and placing it on the table. "I want you to pick this up and toss it behind you."

I'm half tempted to pick it up with my hand, but I know that isn't what he means. Telekinesis on its own is easy. It's combining it with something else that's hard. Instead of being a smart-ass, I focus my mind on the pen. Ballpoint, with blue ink and Silver City University scrawled across the side. The university must have given them out to every student because I have one of my own just like it.

The pen itself isn't heavy as I lift it off the table and press my will into it so hard that it goes flying behind me. Maybe a little more forcefully than I intended based on the resounding *thwack* when it hits the floor.

"Good." He stands, walking past me to go pick up the pen. "Without speaking out loud, tell me which side you'd like your reward. Left or right?"

I hear him as he picks up the pen, his feet shuffling across the floor, but he never appears in front of me again. "I don't—"

"Without words, sunshine."

Letting out a huff, I focus on opening the pathway between our link and push the words to him. *I don't understand.*

"Left or right. Just pick one."

Right.

He must hear my mental response, because he places a soft kiss below my right ear. Electricity races through my body where his skin touches mine, causing the hairs to raise on my arms.

"Here's how this is going to go. If you complete a task, you get a reward. If you don't ... well, let's just say you'll be heading back to your room awfully unsatisfied. Do you agree?" He leans past me, nuzzling into my neck and placing the pen back on the table.

"I do." He's barely touched me at all, yet I can't hide the desperation in my voice. I have a hard enough time focusing on this shit without him seducing me. How the hell am I going to manage now?

"Telepathically from now on, my sweet sunshine." He rests his arms on the back of my chair without touching me, but the warmth of his breath tickles my neck. "Raise that pen a foot above the table and hold it there."

I do as he says, finding the task easier this time now that I know the weight and feel of it. "Very good. Now, keep it there while I help you get a little more comfortable."

Before I can ask him what he means, his hands skate over my shoulders and around to the front of my sweater, then tug slowly on the zipper. The pen wobbles in the air, and I try to fix it but end up over correcting and flinging it off to the side.

Raphael's hands stop unzipping my sweater, and I have to force myself not to whimper. He'd barely moved it at all. *This is hopeless.*

I don't realize that I mentally spoke the words to him until he says, "It's not hopeless, sunshine. Have a little more faith in yourself. You're getting the hang of it far faster than I did when I first learned. Trust your instincts."

He brings the pen back without moving away from me, placing it on the table once more. "Try again."

This time when I clear my mind, I throw away the self-doubt and worries that I'm not good enough and replace it with trust and faith in myself, just as he says. When the pen floats above the table, his hands come back to my sweater. He moves the zipper down ever so slowly, and I can't help the gasp that escapes me when his hands pass over my hardened nipples. The pen wobbles again, but this time, more determined than ever, I don't let it fall.

He pulls the sides of my sweater down to reveal my shoulders to him, where he places soft kisses along their tops, then trails the pad of his tongue up to my ear.

The pen falls to the table with a clatter.

Fuck, I say, mentally.

"Progress is progress. You're doing so good, baby. Don't let it discourage you. Here," he says, pulling on the sleeves of my sweater until my left arm is free. "Let's get you out of this."

With my sweater off, my pebbled nipples are pretty fucking hard to miss, but I try not to think about it. Or all the things I hope he does to them.

We continue practicing for ten minutes, though it feels more like hours. With every successful hold of the pen while he tries to distract me, he rewards me. Sometimes it's only a kiss or a soft touch, but other times he sucks a nipple into his mouth until I think I might come just from that alone. He never lets me get that far, though.

My thighs press together, and I rock back and forth, hoping for more friction. All I want to do is master this stupid fucking power so I can get off.

He leads me to the bed, and I can't help the small skip in my step as he directs me to lie on my back in the center of the bed. With a question in his gaze, his hands move to the waistband of my sweatpants, and I nod vigorously. Is this it? Will he stop this torment and get me off already?

Of course not.

He pulls me to the edge of the bed, placing my feet on the small wooden ledge of the frame, and then stands.

Where are you going? I ask him, sending the question through our mental link because I know that's what he expects.

When I see him grab the pen, I know he's not done torturing me.

"I want you to keep that pen suspended above your head. As long as you do that, I'll feast. Alright?" His eyes are molten silver as he settles on the floor, perched between my legs.

Okay.

My underwear feels slick with arousal, and I wonder if he can tell. *Shit, I'm as wet as a fucking tropical storm. There's no way he won't notice.*

I lay my head back down on the bed and focus on the pen. It hovers above my face — horizontally, so I don't poke my eye out if it falls. When he shifts closer, I feel it. On my calves, my thighs, my core.

Every inch of my skin trembles, needing more of his touch. He kisses a path up my thigh and toward my center, and I strengthen my focus on the pen. When his finger skims over my panties, the pen wobbles, but I catch it before it falls.

Each move he makes is deliberate, building me up slowly so I can reinforce my focus, and giving me the best chance to succeed. I'm grateful, but I'm also horny as fuck.

All this buildup has my body twitching as I inch closer to release. He's pulled my panties to the side and flicks his tongue against my clit. Once, twice, and a third time before he sucks it into his mouth. I'm on the edge, about to shatter into a million pieces, when the pen starts to fall. I catch it before it hits me, lifting it back up above my head, but the damage is done.

Raphael no longer sucks on my clit. In fact, he's barely touching me at all, only watching.

Asshole.

His eyes light up. "What did you just say?"

I called you an asshole.

That's when I realize why he's so excited. The pen still hovers above me and I just spoke to him through our bond. *I did it!*

"That you did, sunshine. And I think you've earned your reward."

He snatches the pen from the air and tosses it over his shoulder before diving between my legs once again. Using his shoulders, he keeps my legs spread wide as he lavishes my oversensitive clit with flicks of his tongue.

One of our slates vibrates, but neither of us moves to answer it. Even if he wanted to, I wouldn't let him. Not when I'm this pent up with need.

My body shakes, so overloaded with pleasure, yet I still don't come. It's like he's held me on the edge for so long that I'm trapped there.

"I'm so close, Raph. Please," I beg, not even sure what I'm asking for anymore.

Raphael's hand inches closer, trailing a path of pure fire until he presses two fingers inside me. He fucks me with them, curving them so they hit that most special place inside me, and I see stars.

A scream erupts from my throat, my hips arching off the bed as one of the most intense orgasms I've ever experienced rushes through me. Raphael keeps torturing me, sparking even more tremors as my pussy spasms around his fingers. I don't realize I've fisted my hands in his hair until the pleasure subsides.

Raphael is nestled between my legs, which are now closed around him to save my poor clit from any more of his delicious abuse. I loosen them, not wanting to choke him after giving me such pleasure.

His smile is wide as he says, "You taste like pure fucking sunlight, baby."

I laugh, not understanding what that even means, though I'm tempted to ask. "Your charm knows no bounds, Raph."

The slate rings again, vibrating from somewhere behind us, and I watch all the joy drain from Raphael's face.

21

RAPHAEL

"What is it?"

Hayliel watches me, her brows drawn together. She sits up, pulling my head from between her legs. With her on the bed and me on the floor, we're almost at eye level.

My slate rings a third time, and I wince.

Hayliel places her hands on my cheeks, cupping them gently. "Raph ... What's wrong?"

My heart speeds up, but as much as I want to dance around the room in utter joy that she's finally using that name, I can't shake the dread that always accompanies thoughts of my family.

"It's nothing," I hedge, hoping to ignore it, but the answering glare from Hayliel spurs me on. "Really, it's nothing. Just my mom calling, most likely. She's not known to give up until I answer, unfortunately."

"Oh."

She says only one word, but it sounds like much more.

"You can answer. I really don't mind. I can step outside if you'd like some privacy?"

"No. Stay, please." I lean forward and place a kiss on her lips. She wraps her arms around me, pulling me into a hug as if she can tell how much I need one.

When we pull apart, Hayliel moves to the head of the bed and begins propping pillows up against the wall, making a cozy place for us to sit.

I reach my slate just as another call comes through. I don't even need to see the word *Mom* flash across the screen to know it's her. The incessant nagging tells me enough already.

With Hayliel here, I consider not putting the call on speaker like I usually would in my room, but brush that thought off. I want her to know me, family shit and all.

Holding my slate, I make my way back to where Hayliel sits on the bed and join her there, the two of us curled up beneath the blankets. I've barely answered the call when my mom's voice rings out.

"Raphael, I thought we talked about this. It's rude to make your mother wait so long."

"Mother. It's a pleasure to hear from you, as always. Sorry for the delay. I'm in the middle of midterm prep with a friend.

We were working on a rather troublesome question when you called."

Hayliel's eyes dance with laughter, and she brings a hand up to cover her mouth.

"Oh, how splendid! Was Theo able to help you solve the problem?"

"Theo is preoccupied at the moment, but Hayliel and I managed to get it right. Speaking of, we should really—"

"A girl! How delightful. Is this Hayliel with you now?" My pulse hammers in my ears as I consider what to say. Do I want my mom talking to Hayliel? I know how awful she can be, but that's usually only directed toward me.

Before I can decide, Hayliel speaks. "I'm here, Mrs. Adams. It's a pleasure to meet you."

"Likewise, my dear. I hope tutoring my Raphael isn't too much trouble. He can certainly be a handful."

I fight the blush rising to my cheeks. Why must my mother talk about me like I'm an ignorant child she's annoyed with? Of course, she never would have considered that *I* might be the one doing the tutoring.

"Actually, it's Raphael who's helping me. If it weren't for him, I'm not sure I'd get through midterms."

"Oh, really? How very interesting. When he was younger, Raphael always struggled with basic subjects. His brother, Raduriel, helped him work through most of it. It's nice to see some of that has stuck."

And there it is. I wondered how long it would take before she brought him up. Less than ten minutes. How unsurprising. Already done with this conversation, I don't bother letting Hayliel or my mother say more.

"We really should get back to studying. Midterms will be here before we know it." I'm not really in the mood to study anymore, but if it will get me off this blasted call, I'll do anything.

"Yes, yes. Go study. We'll chat later, Raphael. Your brother is visiting us soon, and we want to make sure his trip is perfect."

"Of course." The prodigal son returns.

"Nice to meet you, Mrs. Adams," Hayliel calls out, but I hang up before my mother can respond to either of us.

I toss my slate on the foot of the bed and slump down into the mattress, throwing an arm over my eyes. Why must she insist on calling me so often? It would be fine if she had nice things to say or literally anything that wasn't demeaning or praising the great Raduriel. It's not as if I hate her or anything, but I thought coming here would free me from my family drama. That was only a fool's dream.

A soft hand lands on my chest, followed by the press of a warm body curling up against mine. I soak up the support she's offering me, using it to calm my racing mind.

"Is she always like that?" Hayliel asks gently.

I almost don't want to answer her. This topic isn't something I care to talk about often, and certainly not after talking with my mother. "Yes," I say anyway, hoping my short answer will end the conversation.

"I'm sorry."

We stay snuggled like that for a short while. Her head rests on my chest, one arm slung across my middle, and I start to relax.

"I'll be right back," she says before leaving the bed.

I feel her absence immediately. Thoughts of my mother and brother rise to the surface, but I beat them down, remembering the way Hayliel spoke up for me. Who cares what my family thinks when the person I care about, the one with me now, accepts me as I am. With Hayliel, there is no judgment or comparisons.

The sound of her bare feet hitting the floor has me moving my arm off my face, curious to find out what she's doing. My eyes nearly bug out of my head when I find her standing at the edge of the bed, completely naked.

"I realized that I never properly thanked you for such a fine tutoring lesson. If you're up for it, of course."

"What did you have in mind?" I ask, as if it even matters. I couldn't fucking care less at this point. Not when she's undressed and staring at me like a predator eyeing its next meal.

"Why don't you come here and find out?"

I scoot to the edge of the bed, but don't go any further. Even if I wanted to move, I couldn't. The sight before me steals my breath. Her breasts aren't large by any means, but they aren't small either. My mouth waters as I watch her rosy nipples pebble under the weight of my gaze.

She's pulled her hair back into a braid, though a few errant locks have already escaped and now frame her face.

Finally, I look lower to the parts of her I've touched and tasted, but have never fully seen. A small thatch of brown hair sits on her mound, neatly trimmed. I want to taste her again, feel her come apart on my tongue.

She steps closer with purposeful strides, her eyes hooded and heated. As much as I want to reach out to her, I stay still. I had control earlier. It's time to give her the reins.

Her hands go to my shoulders, then up to cup my cheek. "Thank you," she whispers before her mouth descends on mine.

I wrap my arms around her waist, pulling her between my legs as I deepen the kiss. She tastes of honey and sin, and everything else that's good in this world. Her fingers move to my hair, entwining with the strands until she's somehow pulling both away and closer at the same time.

When she breaks the kiss, I'm scared she wants to stop, but she only reaches for the hem of my shirt and pulls it over my head. Instead of returning her lips to mine, she steps back while gripping my pants and guiding me until I'm standing in front of her.

"I can't thank you properly with all these clothes on, Raph."

"Hmm. That does sound like a problem." I smile, not bothering to undress myself. I'd rather she do it for me.

Undeterred, she places kisses along my chest, nipping lightly at one of my nipples before moving lower. When she presses her palm against my jean-covered cock, I can't help but groan.

She chuckles. It's a light, tinkling sound that brings a smile to my face. All I want to do is throw her on the bed and have my wicked way with her. To fuck her on my balcony and lay claim to her for all to see. But I do neither of those things.

As she unbuttons my jeans, she stands on her tiptoes to press a kiss to my lips. Her chest presses into mine, and I roll one of her nipples between my fingers, making her gasp. I swallow the sound, using it to press my tongue into her mouth and deepen the kiss.

She makes quick work of the rest of my clothes until finally I'm standing naked in front of her. We stand still for a moment. There's no pressure to move or do anything as we just take in the sight of each other. Then she grips the base of my cock, pumping slowly as she watches my reaction. She's a quick learner, wasting no time to find out what I like the most.

I feel like a teenager, half a second from blowing my load all over her hand. By sheer force of will alone, I hold off my orgasm.

That's when she drops to her knees in front of me and licks a line from base to tip.

"Hayliel," I gasp, loving the sight of her on her knees.

She cups my balls, trailing kisses along my shaft and stopping to twirl her tongue around the tip every so often until I think I might pass out from all the blood rushing to my cock.

Just when I think she's about to start another round of timid licks and kisses, she wraps her lips around my dick and sucks me into her mouth.

She's warm and wet, and she does this thing with her tongue, pressing it against the sensitive underside of my cock, that has my balls tightening. Fucking hell.

"Touch yourself," I command, wanting her primed and ready for me. For weeks, I've been dreaming about taking her sweet pussy on every surface of my bedroom. It's about time we get started.

She follows my demand seamlessly, her head bobbing and cheeks hollowing out while she sucks the very essence of my being out of me, and begins to stroke her clit.

It's a sight I never wish to forget.

Stay with me tonight.

I don't realize I've pushed the words out until her eyes flash up to mine. She doesn't stop her movements, and I'm only a few pumps away from coming down her throat when she responds.

Okay.

I don't wait another moment before I pull back and reach for her. She comes to me willingly, practically jumping into my arms for a kiss so hot, I'm afraid we might scorch the wood floor beneath us.

But who the fuck cares about wood or floors or anything else when she's in my arms?

Turning us around, I face us both toward my bed and pull the full-length mirror in our direction. We stare at our reflection. She seems so small, yet I know firsthand how strong she is. Her rich olive skin appears far darker than mine, and I can't help but watch as my hands trail over her body.

With barely any effort, I lift her up on the bed, placing her on her knees and stepping up so that I'm flush against her back.

My cock throbs where it rests on her ass, and it takes what little strength I have left not to plunge inside her right now.

Instead, I grip her chin in one hand, tilting her neck slightly so I can kiss a line down it. My other hand goes to her waist and down between her legs. She's wet for me, my fingers coated with her arousal as I push two fingers inside of her and fuck her with them.

"Raphael," she moans, sounding breathless. "If you don't fuck me right now, I swear to the Archangels—"

I chuckle, cutting her off. "There's no need for threats, sunshine." Then I'm pushing inside of her, all the way to the hilt. I watch as her mouth falls open in a silent moan, but don't give her any more time to process. This is what she wanted, isn't it?

One hand curls around her throat, my long fingers crooking over her chin as I tilt her head. "You feel so fucking good, baby," I whisper in her ear. "Do you know how many times I've gotten off to this very image of us?"

She moans as my thrusts turn forceful, my grip on her hips more punishing. She can't see me in the mirror, not with how I'm holding her chin, but I can. And the sight of her lithe body taking every bit of what I offer almost sends me over the edge.

"How many times?" she croaks out, her voice rough.

"Every." *Thrust.* "Fucking." *Thrust.* "Night." *Thrust.*

I let her go, pushing her so she's on her hands and knees. Our eyes lock in the mirror; her face flushed and eyes hooded. Then she's arching her back and pushing into me, meeting every thrust with one of her own.

Her moans grow louder, the walls of her pussy fluttering around my shaft, letting me know just how close she is so I don't let up. I hold back my release, needing her to come with me, to reach bliss in tandem.

Reaching forward, I grab her shoulders and pull her into me with each demanding thrust until she comes, her pussy gripping my cock so hard that I can't help but join her.

We collapse on the bed, not separating from each other. It almost feels as if time is rushing past us. There's a part of me that fears what will happen once we create distance between us. I don't want to break whatever spell we're under. But we can't lie like this forever, can we?

Hayliel groans when I stand, her face shifting into a pout. "Come back to bed, Raph." Her voice comes out muffled where she's buried her face in the blankets.

"We're going to get cleaned up, grab a snack, and then I promise you we'll spend the rest of the evening curled up together, sunshine."

She perks up, her stomach growling. "Did you say food?"

22

HAYLIEL

I've been riding a blissful high all week from the kind words written in the SCU newsletter, but it shatters when I read Theo's message.

Theo: Gagiel's in the infirmary. It sounds like a few students cornered him after class to teach the 'demon lover' a lesson. I don't know much more other than that he's fine and just needs some time to heal.

I've been so focused on what him speaking up meant for me, I never considered what speaking up so publicly in my favor would mean for him.

I don't waste a single second, discarding my studies and throwing on a sweater before rushing to see him. Why hadn't he called me, or even Theo? Maybe the results would have been different if we'd been there.

The front desk of the infirmary is empty, so I ring the bell several times before a rather annoyed-looking angel appears.

"I'm here, I'm here. Quit your dinging. What can I help you with?"

"I'm visiting a patient named Gagiel. I need to see him, please."

The nurse narrows her eyes as she sits down and flips through her chart. "Are you family?"

"No. I'm just a friend."

"Visiting hours for non-family members ends in ten minutes. You'd be better off coming back tomorrow, dear."

"Ten minutes is fine. I just want to make sure he's alright. Please."

She sighs, but stands anyway and motions me to follow her. We don't pass a single other patient or nurse as we make our way through several doors. Gagiel must be lonely in here with no one to keep him company. Resolve settles in my gut. Coming here tonight was the right thing to do.

We stop at the end of a long hallway lit with bright lights when the nurse points to a door held slightly ajar.

"Your friend is in there. Ten minutes, understood?"

"Yes, thank you!"

My hand shakes as I reach for the door. Just how bad are his injuries if he ended up here?

I take a deep breath, steadying myself for the worst, and push the door open.

Gagiel sits on the bed, propped up by several fluffy pillows. His face is red and puffy, and I can see the developing bruises peeking out from beneath his hospital gown, but otherwise he seems unharmed.

He hasn't noticed me yet, his eyes glued to the television secured to the wall across from him. The cooking channel plays reruns of a show my parents used to love watching before the provider started limiting channels on Fallen accounts.

"Hayliel?"

"Are you okay? I came as soon as I heard."

He smiles, the movement pulling at the cut on his bottom lip. "The nurse assures me there won't be any lasting damage, otherwise I'm just tired and sore."

I grab a chair from the corner and bring it to the side of the bed, glad to see that he's doing alright. "Why didn't you call me? We would have come straight away and protected you against whoever did this."

He looks away, picking at the edge of the sheet like he might find the answer there. "They wanted me to call you."

Acid bubbles in my stomach until I feel nauseous. "What?"

"Well, I intended to call you guys as soon as I realized they were waiting for me, but then Cadriel kept making these sly little remarks, like he had a plan for you. I didn't know if they were going to jump you or if they had something worse planned, so I kept silent." He finally looks at me again, and this time there's a little fire behind his eyes. "After everything you've done for me, I couldn't risk you getting hurt."

I grab his hand in both of mine, shocked at the sweet protectiveness of my new friend, even if I'd rather he called me. "Thank you. I appreciate your attempt to keep me safe, even though you shouldn't have had to."

"You would have done the same for me, Hayliel."

"How about this. When you're healed, we can work on strengthening your fighting skills so that if those assholes ever think to attack you again, you'll put them in their place. Deal?"

Gagiel laughs, his brown eyes lighting up. "Deal." He hesitates a moment before sitting straighter and asking, "A few of my friends agreed to come back to campus after midterms. Think you could help them too?"

"Of course! I'm excited to meet them. Plus, now you *must* call me if Cadriel and his idiot buddies ever corner you again, just so I can witness when you pummel their asses."

There's a soft rap on the door before the nurse from the front desk enters. "Visiting hours are over, miss. You can come back tomorrow when curfew's over."

I stand and give his hand one more squeeze, but before I walk through the door, I turn back. "They won't get away with this, Gagiel. I promise you."

A few days later, Theo and I sit together in the Fallen library, flipping through the pages of old books. The nurse released Gagiel from the infirmary, but he's mostly been sticking to his room. Cadriel might live in the house of Power, but he has no shortage of friends.

The library is quiet, with only the faint crackling of old paper as we continue our research. It feels like I've read every single book in here already — including an entire volume on the strict rules and repercussions of Earth-bound travel — but maybe with a fresh pair of eyes, we'll find something.

It doesn't seem to matter where we search. I can't find a single thing about gray-winged angels. There are a few texts that depict other colors, and while I might find that information fascinating, it doesn't help me figure out why I'm different. Could it really be just a fluke?

Raphael was with us earlier, but he had a family crisis to deal with. It sounded like his mother wasn't too happy to hear of our lockdown since he was supposed to go home this weekend to visit his brother. She'd been threatening to contact the principal and demand his release, something Raphael absolutely doesn't want.

He'd rather stay at school than go home, and after what I've learned about his family, I don't blame him. If that was my home life, I'd probably want to avoid it too.

"I still can't believe someone would do something like this."

Theo's smooth voice jolts me out of my thoughts, and I glance up at his look of utter disgust. He holds a book in his hands, and I recognize it as one of the old texts with pages ripped out of it. "This should be a fucking crime."

I laugh. "Seriously! What did that book ever do to them?"

He slams it shut and pushes it away from him like he can't stand the sight of it. "They should have just gotten rid of the whole thing. Tearing out a handful of pages just seems suspicious, doesn't it?"

I nod, realizing he's right. Most of the books were rewritten when the Archangels took over, so why wasn't this one? And why didn't they just pull the entire book from the collection?

"Maybe we'll find the full volume in another library." Theo jots down the title, followed by the words *ripped pages???* before reaching for another book from our stack. The last one on the pile.

We both continue our search, but I can't seem to shake the feeling that I'm being watched. I look up at Theo, whose bright, hazel eyes immediately drop from me to the book in front of him. A few minutes later, I feel the same weighted gaze. Being a little more subtle, I peer up at him from beneath my lashes. Theo watches me, his eyes roaming over me almost appreciatively.

"What?" I ask, wiping my mouth in case I have food stuck there.

"Hm? Oh, nothing. You just ... I like your hair like that."

I bring a hand up to my hair, feeling the smooth strands. Lately, I've been getting tired of it always being in my face, so I've taken to styling it in a half updo. I twisted it a little this morning, but otherwise it's the same style I've been wearing all week.

It's hard to tell in the low light of the library, but I think he's blushing. There isn't much that seems to faze him, aside from demons, so it's cute to see this new side of him. I let my eyes wander down his face and over his fitted black T-shirt. His strength isn't on display like Raphael's, or even Zeke's, but it's there all the same.

"Thanks, Theo. I'll have to wear it like this more often."

I watch as he swallows, smiles, and then turns back to his research. Following along, I flip through the last pages of my own book, but I'd rather watch him. In the weeks since we met, he's never complimented me like that. He always acts so relaxed around me, but now he's jittery and shy, almost awkward even.

Has Raphael told him of our time together? Is this some sort of weird test among friends to see if I'll change my mind and pick the other one?

No. Their bond seems far too strong for that.

An image enters my mind, one of me sandwiched between the two of them, and I can't help the shiver of pleasure that flows through me at the thought. But that's only a dream. Life isn't like that. It's hard to get one happily ever after, let alone multiple. *I swear, some days my mind gets the better of me.*

After not finding anything useful, I grab a few of the discarded books and head back into the stacks. The first few times I came searching in here, I looked for books with specific titles that might prove helpful, but now I just grab books at random.

Who knows what small nugget of information we might find this way? It's not as if being specific has gotten us anywhere.

Before I can grab a few more books, my skin prickles, the little hairs on my arm standing up. It feels different from when I caught Theo staring, yet familiar.

To the left, I spot Theo sitting at the table I just vacated, still engrossed in his book. Behind me there's nothing but shelves, but as I look to my right, I find the culprit.

Zeke glares at me from where he leans against the bookshelves. He's barely a few feet away from me, and I can feel the emotions rushing off him in waves.

"What do you want?" I ask, not bothering to be polite. I'm sick of trying to understand him. Whatever I might have seen in him earlier has vanished, and I don't recognize the asshole underneath.

"Nothing. Just surprised to find you brought them here."

"That's usually what you do with friends. You spend time with them. Not that it's any of your concern. You've made it perfectly clear how you feel about me." Ignoring him, I pluck another book off the shelf.

"Just friends then, are you? Is that what you call all the guys slobbering after you like untrained puppies?"

I can barely follow the conversation when the words escaping him are so confusing. Does he really think I have a lineup of suitors? Is he truly so blind that he can't see Theo and Raphael are the only friends I have outside of Dina?

"Is this really what you want to talk to me about, Ezekiel? Why don't we just get to the point so we can go back to you ignoring me."

His eyes flash a little when I say his full name, but after treating me like shit, we aren't friends. His friends call him Zeke, and I no longer have a seat at that table.

"They're just using you, Hayliel. Don't you see that? It's what they do. A Pure could never actually fall for someone like us, not truly. If you're not careful, they'll stomp all over your heart and leave you to pick up the pieces alone."

For a second, I think he's going to go on. He speaks like he's experienced the very thing he's warning me of, but that can't be true, can it? Can his entire asshole demeanor only stem from his own pain?

The words escape me before I can stop them. "Is that what happened to you?"

Something flashes across his face. Surprise, maybe, or regret? "We aren't fucking talking about me. I know how those Pure assholes work. When they discard you, and they will, don't come crying to me about it."

I can't help but laugh. Is he for real? "We aren't friends, Ezekiel. You made damn sure of that. Since the first day of class, you've either ignored me or glared at me. You don't get to dictate who I spend my time with, and frankly, even if they do discard me, there's no goddamn way in hell I'd be coming to you about anything."

I grab a few more books and turn my back on him, more than done with this conversation. Another thought strikes me then, one I try not to let sink in. In some roundabout way, is he just trying to protect me? I brush it off because even if he is, there are far better ways to go about it.

I only take two steps before I turn around, keeping my voice low. "If you want to spend time with me — without being an ass — you know where to find me."

Once I'm back with Theo, I drop the books onto the table with a loud *thunk*. I can't tell if he overheard us or not, but he doesn't make me wait too long to find out.

"Was that your grumpy house leader?"

"Yup," I reply.

"Want me to kick his ass?"

"Oh, hell no. Stay away from him, Theo. He's a year ahead of us and trained by the Guild. Besides, he's just pissed off at the world and wants to punish me. It's nothing." My heart hammers in my chest at the thought of Theo and Zeke fighting. Theo might be taller, but Zeke has more bulk than even Raphael does. I never want to see them fight.

Instead of saying anything more, he reaches out and grabs my hand, just like I did for him at the assembly. His sweet, minty scent washes over me, smoothing the frayed edges of my mind.

We stay like this for a while, holding hands across the table while we flip through the books I brought over. Neither of us speaks of Zeke again, and as time passes, I feel the weight of that argument slip off my shoulders.

His hands are warm and soft, less calloused than Raphael's, but they still make my blood heat. Thoughts flash through my mind of the two of them. Best friends before I came along, and now I'm drawn to them both.

What the hell have I gotten myself into?

23

HAYLIEL

S nacks? Check.

Sparkling juice? Check.

Opening my slate, I replay the voice message from Dina.

"I'm tired of schooling. Let's just people watch, eat bad food, and gossip today. Meet me in front of the Tower. And bitch, you better not be late."

I laugh at the stern note in her voice. She's been on me all week about how I need to stop stressing about all my problems and just be in the moment. Of course, I told her I would ... once midterms are over.

It's clear she knows me enough to see through my bullshit.

Stuffing everything in my bag, I fly out to meet her. October is finally here, and with it, the crisp scent of fall. Our seasons aren't the same as on Earth. We barely get snow or rain, and our temperatures don't fluctuate, but we still see the leaves turn color and experience a mild shift. Part of me wishes I could steal away down to Earth for a year, just to get the full seasonal experience, but the Archangels only allow a select few to visit, and mostly just to steal their ideas.

"Cutting it awfully close, Hayles," Dina scolds as I land.

"Once you see my snack collection, I think you'll forgive me," I tease. "So, where are we going?"

Dina points up, and I follow the line of her finger until I notice the balcony near the very top of the tower.

"Race you!" I call out, letting my wings free a second later. Dina knows my shit, though, and we make it to the top at almost the same time.

What looked like a balcony from down below is more of a ledge, but there's enough room for us and our bags at least. Dina places a blanket down to cover up the wood, and we both get comfortable with our legs dangling over the edge.

The sun beats down on us, relaxing me all the way to my toes. The sky is clear, not a cloud for miles. It's the perfect weather for a girls' day. From up here, the campus looks so much bigger. There's an almost perfect ring of trees between the main hall and Somersault Falls with a well in the center. I remember seeing it on the map before, but never knew what it was.

"What's that well for?"

Dina glances at the well and shoots me a mischievous grin. "Nothing anymore, but I'm told it's haunted by an angel who fell in and broke her wing. Apparently if you stick your head in at night, you can still hear her calling out for help."

A chill goes through me despite the warm sun. "Like that's not terrifying or anything. If I suddenly go missing, you better be the first person down that well to check for me."

"Duh."

We pull out our snacks and drinks in silence, both content to enjoy the scenery. Dina and I never need pointless conversation. We're too close for that.

It hits me then that I feel the same sense of comfort with Raphael and Theo. It feels weird not to see them today. I can't remember the last day that passed by without at least seeing them in class or afterward.

While we eat, we watch as the students rush around campus. It's clear who the natural loners are from the way they actively avoid other angels. We point out different cliques and their leaders, trying to guess if they'll be in the same groups next semester or if someone else will take their place.

Seraphina and her group of bullies are leaving the main hall and heading off toward the beach. My lips turn down as I think about the cruel things she's said and done to me.

"I hope that group falls apart before next semester. I could use a break from their bitchiness."

"Seraphina is the worst. I dealt with an angel just like her last year. She ended up having to transfer out because of a family emergency, but everyone knew the real reason she left."

"Why?" Curiosity mixes with hope inside me as I wait for Dina to answer.

"She got caught trying to seduce a teacher for better grades. Apparently, she'd already succeeded with a different one in another class, so she thought she'd try her luck again."

I laugh, unable to stop the giggles from bubbling up as I picture Seraphina offering the same. "What happened to the teachers?"

"Not a thing. They didn't have enough proof, and the one professor they caught her with was very clearly not interested. But ..." Dina scans the campus until she spots something. "Do you see that angel there, in the rainbow-colored T-shirt?"

I take another bite of the soft, chewy brownie that I pilfered from the kitchens, holding back a moan of delight before I finally spot the angel Dina is referring to.

All I can manage is a soft "um-hmm" with my mouth full.

"Well, I heard they're fucking a professor. The same one who couldn't keep it in his pants last year."

My mouth practically falls open. "No! Which one?" I ask, trying to imagine which professor gave off those vibes. As angels, we age well, so it's not like the teachers here are ugly, but one thing I've learned is that personality goes a long fucking way in adding, or detracting, from someone's desirability.

"Professor Uriel."

I cringe.

Dina mimics my look before laughing. "I know. If you're going to risk expulsion by fucking a teacher, at least choose one that's not so repulsive."

"Oh, really? And which professor would you choose?"

"Professor Malik," she answers quickly, like she's considered this answer so many times before. "Have you seen the way he moves? Fucking hell. What I wouldn't give to have one-on-one training sessions with that brute of an angel."

Thinking of Professor Malik only brings up memories of Zeke and the way our bodies mold together during class. Honestly, I'd probably have better luck practicing with Professor Malik than I do with Zeke. At least he doesn't hate me.

As if sensing my thoughts, Dina places a hand on my arm. "How are you doing, truly?"

I open a bag of chips, popping one into my mouth while I think about my answer. Dina will know if I lie, but I don't want to burden her with all the raging thoughts spiraling through my head. She won't settle for less though.

"Honestly, I'm a bit of a mess. After spending my entire life close to my parents, it's strange to be so far away from them. Especially now that we're not allowed to leave the campus. I relied on them so much growing up, and now it feels like there's a piece of me missing, ya know?"

"I'm sure they feel the same way. Let's have dinner together with them." She rolls her eyes at the look on my face before elaborating. "We'll have a video call and eat together. I know it's not the same as being in person, but it's close enough for now."

"I'd like that, actually. Thanks, Dina."

"I got you, babe. Besides, I'm sure they're dying to meet Raphael and Theo. Have you told them about your new *friends* yet?" She says the word friends like we're teenagers talking about our newest crush.

"Not exactly."

She throws a peanut at me.

"What am I supposed to tell them when I don't even know what's going on? It's not like Raphael and I have even labeled things, and with Theo ... I *think* he's into me, and I want him to be, but what kind of person does that make me? I don't want to be known as the girl who splits up friends."

"Want my advice?" Dina asks, and I'm half tempted to say no, but I'm not a fool. I trust her judgment more than my own when it comes to angels of the opposite sex.

"Yes," I reply, defeated.

"Let whatever is going to happen, happen. Stop trying to find motives behind every gesture and just let it be. You always get so worked up about the unknown, and that usually blows up in your face. If Theo and Raphael haven't given you any reason to think they're testing you or trying to get you to choose, then stop making them up in your head. Hell, babe, you saw the delicious fucking orgies that happened during the start-of-term party. Maybe your merry band of angels will surprise you."

I can't help the color that rushes to my cheeks at her words. An orgy? With Raph and Theo? I'd fucking expire on the spot.

"See? I knew that would interest you. And for your other admirer—"

"He's not my admirer, Dina. He hates me."

"There's not a chance in fucking hell that angel hates you. I've seen the way Zeke glares at you across the common room. His eyes zero in on you like magnets whenever you're near him. If he wants to be an ass, show him what he's missing, because he *is* missing out on you. He needs to shape up or ship the fuck out."

"Hear! Hear!" I salute her with the bottle of cider before taking a hefty swallow and passing it to her. Dina always knows how to cheer me up or shift my perspective. I'm not sure how I'll show Zeke what he's missing, or even if I'll figure out how to stop stressing so much about Theo and Raph, but something settles inside of me as we sit atop the Tower.

"And what about you? Are there any angels holding your attention, or are you hoping to convince Professor Malik to tangle in the sheets?"

"Well, you know ... he isn't teaching me any classes this semester, so I could probably get away with it."

I slap her playfully. "If you get expelled, Dina, I swear to the Archangels I'll drop out."

"I'm kidding, I'm kidding! Only in my dreams," she says wistfully. "I've actually got my sights set somewhere a little more complicated, if you'll believe it. Remember that throuple on the couch at the start-of-term party? Well, I want to be their fourth."

I almost spit out my drink, and instead end up choking on it as I try to swallow it too quickly. "No fucking way. Dina, that's incredible. When they let you join, I'm going to have a million questions."

"Holy shit," Dina replies, her voice trembling slightly.

"Alright, alright. I won't ask you questions. Sheesh." I'm too busy digging through the snacks for my next treat to catch her expression.

It's only when I look up that I realize why her voice trembled. Along the horizon, a wave of darkness heads straight toward campus.

"Oh shit. Demons!"

24

THEO

It's weird being in the Knowledge library without my usual companions. Hayliel told us that Dina had planned a girls' day for them that was strictly no boys allowed, and Raph's parents wanted him on constant video call since he wasn't able to leave school grounds for his brother's visit.

Instead of studying for midterms — because let's be real, I could ace the tests in my sleep — I continue the search for Hayliel. We've almost made it through every non-fiction book in here, and I'm starting to doubt that we'll find anything at all. But there must be other books somewhere. Despite the Archangels wanting the history books rewritten, it's a rather rash move to destroy everything else.

I checked the library here for any mention of that book with the ripped-out pages, but it's not here. Why would someone leave it in the Fallen library? Why would they rip out any pages at all? It doesn't make sense.

A loud shout breaks through my thoughts, sending my nerves on high alert. Knowledge house is typically the quietest of the three houses. We thrive off information and are more than comfortable spending our weekends nestled up with a good book. As another sound hits me, this time a loud, high-pitched scream, I know something must be horribly wrong.

I make my way toward the tiny vertical windows in the far corner, hoping to catch sight of whatever the fuck is going on. Maybe it's only a group of students playing by the water's edge. *Or maybe it's something far worse.*

My mind races, fear mounting as I press my face to the glass.

Chaos reigns outside as students and faculty run in varying directions, but I can't see anything more than their frantic movements. What the hell is going on?

Panic wells inside me, and I rush out of the library, wanting to find out what has everyone so scared. Before I even make it through the lobby door, though, I see them.

Demons fly toward us like a storm cloud, their massive, bat-like wings seeming to block out the sun and throw us into darkness. One lands inside the gate, rushing directly for Knowledge house. I can't move. As hard as I try, my legs refuse to cooperate. It's like I'm standing in cement that's already dried and all I can do is watch as the demon gets closer, locking in on its target — a student.

In the maelstrom, I can't make out who it is before they take to the sky, doing the exact fucking thing the Guild told us not to. Everyone knows demons are far better in the air than we are. Not that we're weak, but over the course of our history, we've learned the hard way that angels can't outfly demons. Something in their genetic makeup gives them more speed and precision in the air than even we have.

The poor student doesn't make it very far before the demon slams into him and sharp, claw-like wingtips dig into flesh, then the pair fall to the ground in a heap. I want to help him, but I can't make my limbs move. Images and emotions from a time long since passed resurface, consuming everything around me until it's like I'm back there in that skatepark.

I fight the memories back and push out of the lobby and onto the gravel walkway as more demons flood through the academy, tackling the ignorant students trying to flee and fighting them on the ground. Three run straight for me and, just as I fear they'll slice me to pieces, I remember my training.

I dodge their slashes with ease, getting in a few jabs of my own that have the wretched beings snarling with rage. This is wrong. It shouldn't be this easy for me to defend myself, even with as much training and practice as I have.

They take turns attacking me, and it almost feels like they're toying with me. If they wanted me dead, all they'd have to do is attack as a unit. Sure, I'd put up a fight, but without a weapon,

I'm no match for three synchronized demons. As savage as we might think they are, these creatures have just as much training as we do. Why are they going easy on me?

With quick reflexes, I have one of the bastards in a choke-hold as I try to snap its fucking neck while it claws at my arms, leaving deep, red gashes on my flesh. When I succeed, the other two creatures share a glance before rushing off in the other direction. What the hell?

Before I can think about it more, another demon falls from the sky with an angel clasped in its claw-tipped fingers. Blood pools beneath him, the metallic tang tainting my lungs and almost throwing me backward in time to another night just like this one.

Moving on instinct, I knock the demon off before he can deal the killing blow. It roars at me, spittle flying into my face before we face off. There, along the curve of its jaw, is an all-too-familiar scar. Fear climbs through my veins until I step back, but then I blink and the scar is gone. *Fuck. Now is not the time for my mind to be playing tricks on me.*

I steady myself, trying to calm the panic inside before it gets me killed. I dodge a vicious blow but stumble as I twist out of reach. This demon moves differently than the others. His attacks are far more aggressive. Exactly like I'd expect them all to behave. It comes at me with brutal strikes that require every ounce of skill I have just to avoid. If it keeps up like this, I'll tire before it does.

The more we fight, the more the flashbacks threaten to take me under, even though this situation is nothing like the one from when I was fifteen. Maybe it's the demon's violence that reminds me so vividly of that night. The way it swipes its claws through the air, hoping to rip flesh and spill blood.

On the ground, the bloody student whimpers and causes the demon to look his way hungrily, creating a distraction. With no weapon and my memories rushing to the surface, I won't survive this creature. I look around for something I can use, and a barbaric grin spreads across my face. The student wails again, claiming the demon's full focus. Without a moment's hesitation, I act, using the power inside of me to telekinetically uproot a fucking tree and whack him with enough strength that the impact launches him away from us.

Darkness descends, my vision narrowing as I drop to my knees on the grass. My hands feel wet where they rest on the ground, and I struggle to breathe. I wipe them off on my pants, wanting the icky feeling to go away, but that only streaks them with red. Bloody handprints line my jeans, tricking my mind into the past once more. Back to another night with bloody handprints and puddles of red. But this time, it's not pooled beneath some random student. It's her. The angel I got killed.

A warm hand touches my shoulder and I jerk back, throwing a punch toward whatever creature wants to harm me. But what I hear isn't any demon. It's the deep, rich voice that always seems to pull me from my panic.

I blink, trying to clear the fog from my brain, and Raphael finally comes into focus.

"Raph." I tremble like a terrified little boy.

"You hurt?" he asks, checking my body for injury.

"Not physically."

His eyes light up with panic at the sight of the blood on my pants, and I rush to reassure him.

"It's not mine."

"Good. I grabbed this from your room. The entire fucking school needs our help, Theo. Think you can manage it?" He hands me a dagger, the one I never go to sleep without.

I take it from him, relief rushing through me at the familiar feel of it in my grip. With one more deep breath, I stand, feeling more confident now that I have a weapon in my hand.

My friend has his own makeshift weapon. The iron leg of a chair, I think. Or maybe a bench? Whatever it is, I'm glad to see he'll at least be able to defend himself. He can fill me in on where the fuck he got it after we survive. *If we survive.*

"Let's make these fuckers pay."

25

RAPHAEL

A demon shoots from the sky, obliterating one of the benches that surround the bonfire. Motherfucker. It's not that I have any kind of love for that bench, but I had plans to bring Hayliel here after midterms. We would celebrate our victory with s'mores, and I'd finger her beneath the blanket while she'd try to be quiet in order for us not to get caught. Now this asshole demon ruined it.

I dodge one of the creature's long arms, barely avoiding getting cut open by their claws, when another demon lands. Soon, there are five brutes gnashing their sharp teeth at me. One turns away, sensing a group of students rushing to the arena, and suddenly all five of them move to attack the others. What the fuck am I? Chopped liver? These dickheads must enjoy the chase.

Scrambling forward, I grab some of the broken wood and toss it at their backs, hitting one of them on its horned head. They all turn, growls building in their chests. Well, I certainly have their attention now.

I toss one more fragment and end up slapping the closest demon right in the fucking face before picking up the pointed metal leg and running. Thank the Archangels that we're faster on land than they are. But even as that thought surfaces, I turn to find the group of five angry fuckers hot on my tail. *Shit. You need a plan, Raph. Think!*

I rush toward the thickest flower bushes, jumping high to avoid their sharp thorns, and a chorus of grunts comes from behind me as the demons run straight through them. Ha! Suckers. Wheeling around the back of the weaponry building, I head toward the woods, hoping to avoid them until I can figure out a goddamn plan.

When there's a bit of distance between us, I stop beneath an old, thick-trunked tree while I think. The scents of the forest envelop me. Rich and earthy, it settles something inside of me. My balcony overlooks this batch of trees, and I've studied it enough to know how to get out of here unseen.

I try not to think of Hayliel or Theo, but the harder I try, the more I worry. Are they safe? Or has one of these beasts already got to them?

A twig snaps somewhere behind me, and I brace myself for a fight. When I turn to attack, though, I don't find any demon.

"Fucking hell," Dina whisper-shouts, backing up before my bench leg can make contact with her skin.

Relief floods through me, quickly followed by frustration. "Didn't anyone teach you not to approach an angel who's trying to avoid a horde of demons?"

"I saw you rush in here with five of them on your tail. Hayliel would fucking kill me if I let anything happen to you, dick."

At the mention of her name, my face falls. "Where is she? Is she okay?"

Before she can answer, one of the demons spots us. It rushes toward us, stumbling over tree roots and stumps, but nothing stops it. That dude will have a fuck ton of bruises after today. And even more once we're done with it.

Weaponless, Dina throws a massive rock at it before darting to the side and holding every ounce of the demon's attention. She dodges three swipes of its claws before landing a punch of her own that nearly sends the creature crashing to the floor. It only enrages the beast further.

Dina smiles, her face filled with what I can only describe as joy. I swear she even lets out a little giggle as she continues to avoid any damage while dealing plenty in return. When the demon finally lands a hit, scraping one of its claws across her arm, Dina growls.

"You're going to fucking pay for that."

While the beast is distracted, I creep forward, ready my strike, and swing the iron leg. I hit him right in the ear, the metal screw piercing through his head in a sickening crunch. It turns to me, takes one half-assed swipe, then crumples to the forest floor.

Unfortunately, this won't kill it. Only a sun blade can truly manage that, but this not-so-little beastie will be down and out for enough time that we can hopefully find our friends.

"Hayliel?" I ask again, tearing my trusty bench leg free from the demon's skull before turning to Dina.

"We were together on the Tower when they came. We got separated after that."

"Fuck. I haven't seen her or Theo yet. Want to track them together, or should we split up?"

She's weaponless, aside from her combat skills, which are clearly good enough to survive, so I'm not surprised when she says, "Split up. You go find Theo, and I'll look for Hayliel. Meet back at the fountain?"

I nod, not wanting to waste any more time. "Stay safe," I call out, then rush off through the trees.

Exiting the forest, I end up in front of the house of Power. To my surprise, there aren't any demons or angels in sight. Only destruction. Of all the statues that usually line the path here, only one remains while the rest lie in chunks on the grass.

I stick to the front gate, moving swiftly toward Knowledge house, which is where I hope to find Theo. He was supposed to be studying in the library, but I'm going to check his room first.

With so many demons around, I can't imagine how he's faring. I just have to hope his panic hasn't left him an easy target.

Sneaking around the side of Knowledge house, I work my way toward Theo's balcony. I'll need to fly to access it since I don't have a key. Thank the Archangels we coded our wings to unlock each other's rooms.

I barely get in the air when a force slams into me.

All the breath leaves me as I'm knocked to the ground by a demon so thick, I'm surprised my ribs haven't caved in. The bench leg I was holding lies abandoned and out of reach. Before I can steady my breathing, the monster attacks and I barely avoid the dagger-like claws that now drive into the dirt.

The idiot has its hand stuck in the ground, giving me just enough time to skip around it and grab my weapon. I let out a manic laugh, my heart pounding in my ears as I take aim and slam the screw into its eye. The victory is short-lived when the fucker swipes out and slices my legs, ruining my favorite pair of jeans in the process, before shuddering to the ground with a thud.

I don't waste any time flying as quickly as I can to Theo's balcony before letting myself into his room.

But he's not here.

The weapon I find beneath his pillow tells me he hasn't been up here since the attack. Where is he? He doesn't have a weapon. His past still has a chokehold on him. Shit.

I race to the library, hoping to find him tucked safely away in a corner, but the room is empty. In fact, the space looks entirely untouched. Maybe the demons didn't make it over here yet. But where else could he be?

Not really sure where to look next, I head out of the library and toward the front entrance. The door is swung wide, almost broken off its hinges, and the echoes of a scream ring from somewhere in the distance.

The area outside the house is a ruin of broken siding and bodies. I check on the wounded, happy to find all of them still alive. When I reach the last body, he croaks out words that are almost unintelligible, but I can make out two of them. "Saved me." He points somewhere off to the left, and that's when I see it.

Theo sits on his knees in the grass, practically curled into himself.

After scanning the area for demons and finding none near enough for me to worry about, I race toward him. Given his current predicament, I should probably have approached with a bit more care because when I touch his shoulder, he thrashes and turns to hit me.

"Whoa," I say gently, as if speaking to a spooked horse. "It's me. You're safe. I've got you."

Theo blinks a few times before his tense shoulders relax beneath the grip of my fingers.

"Raph."

"You hurt?"

He lets out a long breath. "Not physically."

His hands are bloody, and my mind immediately goes on high alert, scanning him for injury.

"It's not mine," he reassures me. It must be the blood of the student he saved. He has no weapon though, so I don't know how the fuck he managed that.

"Good. I grabbed this from your room. The entire fucking school needs our help, Theo. Think you can manage it?" I hand over his dagger and watch as his eyes change, shifting into something the demons should be afraid of.

He stands with more confidence than I've seen in his movements in a long-ass time, and I know it's from the dagger he holds. He eyes my weapon skeptically, but this fucking bench leg is nothing to be scoffed at. My trusty sidekick hasn't let me down yet.

"Let's make these fuckers pay."

I nod, eyeing the demons as they swarm the skies. Predators, searching for their next prey. Not fucking today, dickwads.

"Have you heard from Hayliel?" Theo asks.

"No. I saw Dina though. She said they got separated. I came for you and she went in search of Hayliel, but we're supposed to meet at the fountain. We should head there now."

His eyes scream with the same distress I feel. We just have to hope to all that's holy that Dina was able to find her unharmed.

We head toward the fountain, searching the land and sky for any potential attack. As we pass by the door to the main hall, every demon stops what they're doing, turning all at once to face the front gate. What the ...

"Are they retreating?"

"Maybe ..." Theo replies, his quiet voice full of skepticism. His demeanor shifts into something I've seen more times than I can count. He closes his eyes, focusing hard on forcing the flashbacks away and not letting them take over.

"Hayliel needs you, Theo. We need to find her and protect her. Don't let those assholes win." I place my hand on his shoulder, pushing my own strength into him until I feel his muscles relax, and he opens his eyes.

He shoots me a nod before surveying the demons again.

With my mind on high alert, I walk around the side of the main hall and finally catch sight of the fountain, but Dina and Hayliel are nowhere to be found. Fuck!

Propped up against the fountain are two students, each with bloody wounds, but they'll survive. Theo joins us, tearing off a piece of fabric from the guy's shirt before pushing it onto the wound and applying pressure.

"Have two angels come this way, one with black wings and one with gray wings?"

"No. Just those monsters," the more coherent one says. He shudders, then winces as the movement rubs against his wounded shoulder.

Just as I'm about to ask Theo if he has any ideas for another plan, something tugs at my mind. A familiar brightness, one I would recognize anywhere. Hayliel.

Something's wrong. Spinning frantically, I search the grounds for any sign of my sunshine, or at least something to tell me where her signal came from.

Before I can speak up, Theo says three words that have my fear spiking.

"They aren't retreating."

"Where are they going?" I don't doubt his words for a second. Not after all the research he's done on these creatures. He's the expert in this situation. We watch as all the demons, airborne and on the ground, converge toward one location. The ring of trees surrounding the well.

"I think they're targeting the biggest threat."

My stomach drops as I push my mental energy toward the area. No ... it can't be.

"Hayliel's there," I whisper. Sound fades into the background until I can only hear the blood rushing through my veins. Like a shot, we both take off. Are we fools for rushing toward a swarm of angry demons? Probably. But we'd follow our angel to the pits of fucking Hell. No one will take her from us.

We run and run, pushing ourselves hard to reach the well, not daring to fly with so many of the creatures there. At this rate, though, we'll never make it in time.

Something inside of me splinters at the thought of her alone against such a massive horde, and there's nothing I can do about it. I can't save her. I suck in a lungful of air and call out to her, needing her to know she's not alone.

"Hayliel!"

26

EZEKIEL

The city is quiet as I leave the Guild after a rather grueling day of admin tasks. As an intern, it's required that I assist members with varying degrees of tasks so that I can fully understand what being part of the Guild truly means.

Not that I hate paperwork, but with so much shit going on, it seems almost pointless. We're constantly responding to demon sightings or attacks, but it's like they're always one step ahead of us. Who the fuck cares about filing when there's something far greater that needs our attention.

Of course, I don't tell my lieutenant that. I'm not an idiot. Any sign of complaint and he'll ensure I have that task and *only* that task for weeks, so I put my head down and keep my lips zipped. That little plan worked out in my favor because I'd finished early and was allowed to leave. From the sheer number of Guild members rushing about, I must have been the only one not assigned more tasks. It's my lucky day.

The sun beams down on my black wings as I soar through the sky, relaxing me as I fly toward the campus. It looks different from up here, less shiny and perfect than I remember.

It's only when I fly a little closer that I realize why. SCU is under attack!

Tucking my wings, I dive toward the ground until I'm about to faceplant. Only then do I spread my wings again. I land outside the front gate, my feet slapping the pavement with a sound so loud, I hope to fuck I don't attract any demons. There'll be time to fuck them up, but first I have to get the Guild here ASAP.

The Guild uniform has a mini slate built in that attaches to an earpiece. It's a clever little gadget and saves us from carrying around the larger slates that might slow us down. As long as the small devices don't get hit directly, they work perfectly.

I dial the on-duty lieutenant line first, hoping to hear Azrael's voice, but no one responds. After a few more calls to him go unanswered, I try the regular emergency line, which usually guarantees that someone will pick up, but it only rings endlessly. Trying again, I watch the demons through the iron bars of the fence.

They're vicious creatures, content only when they're covered in the blood of angels, but something about the way these demons move makes me wonder if that's true.

I watch one as it catches an angel from the sky and forces them to the ground, using the angel as a fucking hammer to break one of the Knowledge house's statues. I can hear the fucking bones shatter from here, but the demon doesn't deal a killing blow. It snarls once, twice, and then moves on to another target.

What the fuck is going on?

After yet another call goes unanswered, I realize I can't just stand on the sidelines and wait for the cavalry to arrive.

They aren't fucking coming. At least I can help protect others from harm, even if I can't kill the invaders fully.

It isn't the first time I've wished the Guild would let interns carry a sun blade.

Not wasting another second, I run headfirst into the fray. Thank the Archangels that I always wear my full gear when I head to the Guild, or I'd be shit out of fucking luck.

Whoever makes the tech for us is one smart-ass angel. They've created a weapon that changes with the press of a button. If I need a sword, I only have to press the button and push my want into it. If I want a bow, I do the same. It's one hell of a multipurpose weapon.

Drawing an arrow from the quiver on my back, I take aim with my bow and let it fly. Bullseye! It hits a demon in the back of the skull, and I watch as it collapses to the ground.

Unfortunately, the damn beast let out a shriek before it fell and now I have three demons rushing toward me. I pop off one more arrow, hitting my target in the stomach before I change the weapon into a long-bladed sword. The weight of it feels perfectly balanced in my hand, and I move on practiced steps as I parry and strike against my opponents. Their claws strike the metal, causing sparks to fly, but I ignore them and stab my blade through the chin and skull of one dark creature before focusing on the other.

Professor Malik makes a stand on the front lawn, tearing through the creatures with ease. He holds a pair of twin daggers, slashing and blocking as the demons advance before dispatching of them. There's a lull in attacks, and I take the opportunity to approach him.

Seeing my uniform, his face lights up. "Good, the Guild is here."

I cringe. "Not exactly. I've been trying to reach someone at HQ, but no one's picking up."

"Fuck! Principal Cael said as much. We need more manpower, or at least more weapons in the hands of our students."

Professor Malik's head whips around when someone cries out near the house of Power. "I've got to go. Take down as many as you can and hopefully that will buy us enough time." Then he turns his back on me and rushes into battle.

I fight on toward the main hall, struggling to understand how so many of these beasts made it through our defenses, when the largest demon I've ever seen lands on the ground in front of me.

It stands over seven feet tall, with scaly wings that span wide along its back and nearly block out the rest of the world.

Where the fuck is the Guild?

I dart left to avoid a wicked slash of claws, miscalculating the beast's long arms as it tears into my uniform, but thankfully doesn't hit flesh. It may be large, but on the ground it's slow. On quick feet, I'm able to dance around it, jabbing and cutting several times until a stream of black blood oozes from the wounds.

The demon reaches back, winding up for a massive attack, when suddenly it falters. It's like watching a windup toy run out of steam and waiting for your dad to come wind it up again. Finally it moves, but not to attack me. It turns and runs in the opposite direction.

My blood turns to ice. I've read documents on this strange behavior — of demons following some silent command that only they can hear. But if the Guild hasn't shown up yet and there's only staff and students here, where the fuck are they going?

I try calling my lieutenant once more, hoping that he'll finally pick the fuck up. We need him and the Guild here. With the way the demons are now converging to one area, who knows how bad things are about to get?

When he doesn't answer, I can't stop the overwhelming feeling of being let down. I try calling my dad, knowing that if he doesn't answer my calls, then something really fucked up must be going on.

He doesn't pick up.

Sheathing my weapon, I race after the demons, hoping to find out what the fuck they're running toward. Hayliel's little friends rush in the same direction. They should be inside somewhere. Hell, they should be protecting *her*.

The blond one carries a tire iron or something — not exactly a great weapon against demons — and the other one has a dagger. Just great. We're so fucking unprotected that we now need Pures to defend and protect us.

I'm seconds away from calling out and telling them to get the fuck inside when the blond one looks around, panicked. It's only when his gaze flashes toward the crop of trees surrounding the well that I begin to worry myself. They take off in a mad dash, heading straight for the spot where the demons gather.

I'm not exactly sure why I follow them. Maybe it's because I'm better trained than they are and I don't want to see anyone else get hurt. Or maybe it's something else, something related to Hayliel and far too mushy, that I don't even want to admit.

Either way, I'm drawn toward them, following as their steps turn more frenzied. The blond one shouts, and I realize what we're all racing toward and who we're already too late to save.

"Hayliel!"

She stands at the top of the hill near the well, her gray wings completely closed around her body. At least twenty demons swarm around her, closing the distance with each passing second. Even with our speed, we'll never make it in time to save her.

I've let her down again, and this time, I might not have the chance to make it right.

27

HAYLIEL

Pain jolts through my body like a lightning strike as I hit the ground with a thud. Fuck.

A small, jagged rock digs into my side, and my mind feels like a bowl of soggy oatmeal. I struggle to catch my breath. The pieces are finally coming together when I spot the two creatures who drove me from the sky.

I guess this explains why Lieutenant Azrael told us not to fly.

From my place on the ground, the demons look massive. When I get to my feet, I realize they don't just look huge, they *are* huge. I might have thought Raph, Theo, and Zeke were tall, but next to these assholes they look like children.

Other than a few sketches, I've never seen a demon before. Survivors of their attacks are few, outside of the Guild anyway, but they appear almost like the love child of a dragon and a bat. And maybe something else too, but I probably shouldn't just lie here ticking off animals in my head.

Shit. How the fuck am I supposed to get out of this situation?

Where's Dina flown off to? I haven't seen her since I fell from the sky. Even then, I'd only caught her zipping off toward the other side of campus before two demons took chase. I hope she's alright.

Off in the distance, Professor Castiel fucking pummels a demon to the ground. As expected, he dances gracefully through the moves, dodging and striking, but it's the power behind his movements that catches me off guard. *Not everything is as it seems, huh, Professor?*

Around me, demons hover in the sky, taking out any angel who tries to flee while others battle on the ground. It's absolute chaos. Try as I might, I keep hoping I'll find someone wearing the Guild uniform. They should be here soon, I'd imagine. It's their job to protect us, after all.

My hands feel empty as I scramble backward, keeping my wary gaze trained on the two demons advancing toward me. The fall must have jarred my brain, because I can't help but want to laugh at the way their giant forms stumble across the rocks and dirt.

An idea flashes in my head, one that's probably foolish since I doubt I'll be able to pull it off, but I have to try. With my back to the campus entrance and the main hall on my left, I find a boulder near the line of trees on my right. My first attempt to move it proves unsuccessful, but when I try again, I can feel it shift. *Almost got it.*

Triumph flows as I hurl the rock toward the closest demon with all my might. But instead of the massive slab of earth I expect to hit it, a handful of fist-sized rocks ping off its enormous frame.

The beast lets out a sound that has my hackles rising. Is it … laughing at me? The demon I hit with my pebbles turns to the other one, the odd gurgling sound growing louder. *Okay, rude.*

Using their momentary distraction, I try to figure out a game plan. If they're this slow on land, how much worse will they be in water? I need to get to Somersault Falls, but first I have to lose these two laughing fucktards.

I might not be able to use my angelic gifts properly in a fight, but I think I've learned enough in combat class to take these fuckers down. The more I believe it, the more likely it'll be true, right? Manifestation and the power of positive thinking. Let's hope it works, or I'll be demon chow in a matter of minutes.

With a rush of speed, I spin, arching to the side and slamming my heel into the knees of the first demon. The laughter turns sour as its knees hit the dirt, finally bringing it to a level I can reach to punch it in its stupid, smug face.

I haul back my arm, fist locked, and throw my punch right as the demon swivels its head to look at me. There's a sickening crunch and blinding pain in my hand, but the asshole falls to the ground in a heap.

The second demon doesn't let me have my victory dance, advancing toward me with a snarl. *Not laughing now, are we, Mr. Bigshot?*

It swipes a claw-tipped hand my way, but I dance out of reach with an almost gleeful snort. Zeke might hate me, but damn can that angel teach. I feel invincible, like every ounce of grueling training we've done over the past few weeks is finally paying off.

The thought is short-lived, however, when I get a little too cocky. Instead of falling for my tricks again, the demon anticipates my movement and lands a cutting blow to my thigh. Blood oozes from the wound, coating my leggings. Fucker! These were my comfiest pair.

I let out a shriek of indignation before coming at the creature with everything I have. This time, I don't bother trying to trick it with fake moves. I overwhelm it. A punch to the gut has it keeled over, the perfect position for me to throw a dirty elbow into its angry face.

I put as much force into it as I can, surprising myself when the demon literally gets air and crashes into the bushes in front of the main hall.

Holy shit. I can do that?

Not wanting to waste any more time, I tuck that little nugget of information away for later. If I survive, I'll think on my wicked strength tomorrow, but for now, I have to get to the water.

I take one more glance around campus, hoping to find ... something. The Guild? Demons retreating? I don't know. But what I don't expect is the horde of snarling monsters heading straight for me. Some are in the sky, flying faster than my eyes can track, while others lope across the ground on massive legs.

Fuck, I can't fight off twenty demons at once. I need help!

I duck into the ring of trees next to me, racing up the hill toward the Falls. If I can just make it there, maybe I'll be alright. But I only make it to the crest of the hill near the old well when I'm surrounded.

Demons drop from the sky, joining their friends as they close in on me. What the fuck do I do? They didn't teach us this shit. Hell, we were told to leave the fighting to the trained members of the Guild, but where the fuck are they?

Fuck, fuck, fuck!

Fear wells up inside me, bubbling over and taking me to my knees. As if on instinct, my wings escape from my back, curling around me until I'm wrapped in a cocoon.

I try to slow my breathing, to think of a plan ... anything to get me out of here alive. I'm not ready to die, and I definitely don't want to be torn apart by fucking demons when I do.

A sound filters in through the walls of my wings. It's faint, muffled by the feathers, but it sounds like my name. When I hear it again, I know without a doubt that there's someone out there calling for me. Is it a trick? A mind game played by those beasts to get me out of my protective cage?

"Hayliel!"

This time, I recognize the voice. But it isn't just one voice, it's multiple. Raphael and Theo call for me, sounding almost pained. Then I hear Dina's voice and even, to my surprise, Zeke's. They sound worried. For me.

Something shifts inside me. I have people that care about me. I'm not alone, and my friends are out there with those creatures. They could get hurt, or worse. How many angels have those monsters taken from us already today? No fucking more.

Burning anger washes away the fear, and my muscles tense as I strain to hold in my rage. But if holding back means the angels I care about get hurt, I won't.

All at once I stand, unfurling my wings on a scream that seems to come from the very depth of my being. Light flashes bright behind my eyes, and I almost collapse to the ground. As the light fades, I'm left panting, limbs shaking, and not entirely sure what the fuck just happened.

The twenty demons that surrounded me before are gone. Ashes lie in their wake, floating on the breeze and coating the grassy hill in soot. Without meaning to, I let a piece of it fall into my hand, not fully understanding what's going on.

The beat of my heart roars in my ears, growing louder while my brain tries to catch up. But it's not my heart making that noise. Tearing my gaze away from the smoldering remains, I find my classmates staring at me in open-mouthed shock. It's not a look I'm used to seeing. There's no disdain or anger on their faces. Instead, it almost looks like awe. But why? I hid beneath my wings like a coward. I couldn't protect myself, let alone anyone else.

Where had that bright light come from, and how the fuck did it destroy the demons?

No one speaks. No one moves. I search the crowd of onlookers for the familiar faces of my friends. They had been calling for me, right? Or was that all a dream?

If anyone will tell me what the fuck happened here, it's them. They won't lie to me.

I'm exhausted and half tempted to curl up on the soft hill for a nap when I finally spot Zeke standing with Raphael and Theo. I sure as hell didn't expect to see them together.

They push through the crowd, their steps faltering when they see me.

I tilt my head, wondering what the fuck they're staring at when Raphael speaks out, answering my internal question. Shit. I didn't mean to send that thought to him. I'm a fucking mess.

"Well, sunshine. It seems your nickname fits." He smiles, but I don't feel any better. In fact, now I'm even more confused than before.

My mind spins, pistons firing as his words begin to click, but before I can put everything together, Zeke's husky voice rings out.

"Your wings, hummingbird. They're ... gold."

I want to laugh, because his words don't make sense. My wings aren't—

Sure enough, when I glance over my shoulder, I find my wings are no longer gray. They're golden, almost glowing against the light from the setting sun.

What the hell?

A few professors have now joined the fray at the base of the hill. No one approaches me and the pile of ashes at my feet. They only whisper and stare.

As if I wasn't different enough already ...

Hayliel's story will continue in *Wings of Torment*.

Acknowledgements

Thank you so much to Charlotte Black at CB Editing Services and Lauren from the Eclectic Editor for making this story shine. Thank you to my wonderful friend Darcy for agreeing to beta read. I'd have been in quite a pickle if you hadn't caught that year 2 snafu!

Thanks to all my friends who kept me going these last few months. You know who you are.

Thanks so much to Cassie from Opulent Designs for making this cover everything I hoped it could be.

Thank you to my nugget queen bestie Cici Reads for being my hype queen. You always make me feel like a million bucks and I can't express how much that means to me.

Thank you so much to Pretty Little Images for pumping out such incredible graphics, and to Aestheteam Designs for the beautiful headers and breakers.

Thank you to my dear friend and PA Megan. This story might not have made it without you.

Thanks to hubby, my real life book boyfriend, for supporting me and picking up the chores I let drop.

And finally, thank you to all the readers who took a chance on me. Without you, this wouldn't be possible.

About the Author

Victoria is a Canadian girl with a love for travel, music, books, games, and mayonnaise. She spends her mornings writing before work, and hopes to one day write full time. Friends say she gives the best hugs and you can usually find her laughing at her own lame jokes.

Facebook Group: /victoriasvillainousqueens

Facebook: /victoria.pauley.506

Instagram: @victoriapauley.author

TikTok: @victoriapauleyauthor

Linktree: /victoriapauley

Website: victoriapauley.com

Also By Victoria Pauley

Standalones

Caged *(MF Gang Romance)*

A Night of Indulgence and Sloth *(MFM, Office, Dark Romance)*

Series and Duets

<u>Silver City University</u>

(RH/Why-Choose, Academy, Paranormal Romance)

Wings of Deception

Wings of Torment

<u>Creating Destiny Duet</u>

(Double MF Fantasy Romance, Greek Mythology)

Guided by the Stars

Fighting for the Stars